ISLAMIC
BELIEFS AND PRACTICES

THE ISLAMIC WORLD

ISLAMIC
BELIEFS AND PRACTICES

EDITED BY MATT STEFON, ASSISTANT EDITOR, RELIGION

Britannica®
Educational Publishing

IN ASSOCIATION WITH

ROSEN
EDUCATIONAL SERVICES

Published in 2010 by Britannica Educational Publishing
(a trademark of Encyclopædia Britannica, Inc.)
in association with Rosen Educational Services, LLC
29 East 21st Street, New York, NY 10010.

First Edition

Britannica Educational Publishing
Michael I. Levy: Executive Editor
Marilyn L. Barton: Senior Coordinator, Production Control
Steven Bosco: Director, Editorial Technologies
Lisa S. Braucher: Senior Producer and Data Editor
Yvette Charboneau: Senior Copy Editor
Kathy Nakamura: Manager, Media Acquisition
Matt Stefon: Assistant Editor, Religion

Rosen Educational Services
Joanne Randolph: Editor
Hope Lourie Killcoyne: Senior Editor and Project Manager
Nelson Sá: Art Director
Matthew Cauli: Designer
Introduction by Janey Levy

Library of Congress Cataloging-in-Publication Data

Islamic beliefs and practices / edited by Matt Stefon.—1st ed.
       p. cm.—(The Islamic world)
"In association with Britannica Educational Publishing, Rosen Educational Services."
ISBN 978-1-61530-017-4 (library binding)
1. Islam—Customs and practices. 2. Islam—Doctrines. I. Stefon, Matt.
BP174.I87 2010
297—dc22

                                                                    2009038290

Manufactured in the United States of America

On the cover: The Qur'an, the sacred scripture of Islam, is for Muslims the word of Allah
(God) as revealed to the Prophet Muhammad. The word Qur'an (also spelled Koran) is
Arabic for "recitation." *Boryana Katsarova/AFP/Getty Images*

CONTENTS

INTRODUCTION

Islam is and has for centuries been one of the world's most important and influential religions. Today, it is the second largest religion on Earth, with more than one billion followers around the globe. Yet most Westerners know and understand little about it. If the September 11, 2001, terrorist attacks on New York City and Washington, D.C., thrust Islam into Western consciousness, they certainly did nothing to improve the Western world's understanding of it. Listening to most news stories reported in the United States since the attacks, one could easily form the misperception that most Muslims are violent extremists bent on destroying Western civilization and imposing strict Islamic fundamentalism on the world. Yet this is a distortion that paints a grossly inaccurate picture of Islam and dishonors the vast majority of Muslims. So then what exactly is Islam? What is its history? What are its teachings?

Islam—like Judaism and Christianity—revolves around belief in the one and only God, whom Muslims call Allah. At the heart of Islam is the notion of *tawhid*, or the oneness of God. The Qur'an, Islam's holy book, constantly stresses Allah's reality, unknowable mystery, and actions on behalf of his creation. Also stressed are Allah's many names, including Lord of the Worlds, the Most High, the One and Only, the Living One, the Sublime, the Wise, the Omnipotent, the Merciful, and the Constant Forgiver. For Muslims, nothing happens in the world unless Allah wills it. Thus, one often hears the phrase *insha'a Allah*, which means "if Allah wills," in Muslims' daily conversations. The believer's relationship to Allah is expressed in the very name of the religion. Islam is an Arabic word meaning "surrender."

Muhammad—known to Muslims as the Prophet Muhammad or simply the Prophet—founded Islam. He was born around 570 in the city of Mecca, in what is today Saudi Arabia. An important commercial center, Mecca was also a preeminent pilgrimage site because of the Ka'bah, a shrine central to the religious cults of various Arab tribes and decorated with cult idols.

Muhammad's parents belonged to the Quraysh, Mecca's ruling tribe and guardians of the Ka'bah. It would seem he was destined to have a secure position in Arab society. However, tragedy struck before he was even born. His father died, leaving his mother to raise him. Following established custom, she sent the infant to live with a desert family so that he might learn the purest Arabic, Arab traditions, self-discipline, nobility, and freedom. According to Muslim tradition, it was during this period that something astonishing happened. Two angels appeared to the young Muhammad, purifying his heart with snow. Soon after, the boy returned to his home.

Back in Mecca, tragedy struck again. Muhammad's mother died when he was six years old. He then went to live with his grandfather, who died two years later. The young Muhammad moved once again, this time to live with his uncle Abu Talib, the father of 'Ali. In spite of all the tragedy he had experienced, Muhammad grew to be a remarkable young man. By the time he was 24, he was running his uncle's business and was renowned for his honesty, fairness, and generosity. The people of Mecca called him al-Amin, "the Trusted One," and often sought his help in settling disputes. He was a highly respected figure in Mecca by the time he was 35.

Muhammad's reputation owed much to his deep religious devotion. He often went into the desert to pray and meditate. On one of these desert trips, around 610, Muhammad received a visit from the archangel Gabriel. This event marked the beginning of the revelation of the Qur'an, which Gabriel delivered to Muhammad from Allah. The revelations continued until shortly before Muhammad's death in 632.

Muhammad shared the revelations first with his family, then with a few friends. Three years after Gabriel's first appearance to him, Muhammad started preaching publicly. He soon attracted followers, including some of Mecca's most distinguished residents. However, most prominent Meccans, as well as some members of his family, rejected Muhammad's teachings, partly for practical reasons. For the Prophet and his followers, Mecca's great shrine, the Ka'bah, had been built by Adam to honor the one God and rebuilt later by the Jewish prophet Abraham. People of Mecca feared that such teachings, combined with Islam's renunciation of idolatry, would drive away the pilgrims who came to the Ka'bah—and the influx of money they brought with them. As Muhammad's influence grew, opposition to him increased.

In 619, Muhammad experienced more tragedy as well as a profound spiritual event. The tragedy lay in the deaths of his first wife and his uncle Abu Talib. The spiritual experience occurred when he fell asleep while visiting the Ka'bah one night. The archangel Gabriel took Muhammad to Jerusalem on a winged horse. There, they ascended through the higher stages of being. Muhammad finally arrived before the throne of Allah, where he received the supreme treasury of knowledge and the final form and number of the Islamic daily prayers. This experience became known as the Mi'raj.

Persecution against the Prophet and his followers increased, making Mecca dangerous for them. Then, in 621, Muhammad was invited to move to Yathrib, become the city's leader, and help solve the political and social difficulties plaguing the city because of its diverse population. After some consideration, Muhammad agreed. He and his followers completed the Hijrah, or migration, in 622, and Yathrib became known as Madinat al-Nabi—City of the Prophet—or Medina. On the outskirts of the city, Muhammad ordered Islam's first mosque to be built. He also created a constitution for the troubled city. This constitution is of great importance to Muslims, who believe the Prophet created the ideal Islamic society, one based on social justice, in Medina.

Islam continued to grow, and eventually all Medina's Arabs became Muslims. Muhammad died in 632, after a final pilgrimage to Mecca to visit the Ka'bah.

The revelations Muhammad began receiving in 610 constitute the Qur'an. The holy text is written in Arabic, Islam's sacred language. For Muslims, Arabic is essential for conveying Allah's message since it was the language Allah chose. This means that, although the Qur'an has been translated into many languages, only through the original Arabic can one truly know Allah's message.

The Qur'an consists of 114 chapters called suras, each of which is divided into verses called *ayahs*. Each sura has a title, and Muslims believe Muhammad named the suras following instructions from Allah. Muslims hold that Allah revealed the arrangement to the Prophet.

Arab culture in Muhammad's day emphasized the spoken word over the written one. Muslims believe that, like many of his contemporaries, Muhammad could neither read nor write. Thus he dictated the revelations to scribes—word for word and sentence by sentence—exactly as he received them, without altering a single word. The spoken word remains important for modern Muslims, too. Most contemporary Muslims are not Arabs and do not know Arabic; also, many Arab Muslims are illiterate. Yet they know passages from the Qur'an. Many Muslims even know the entire Qur'an by heart.

The Qur'an is considered a book of instruction and guidance. It relates the qualities of Allah but also emphasizes the importance of reason. It offers commentary on the meaning and implications of human history as well. In addition to the instruction contained in the Qur'an, Muhammad's life provides an example for Muslims to imitate. His words and actions are known as the Sunnah, and tales about him are collected and preserved in the Hadith. Unlike the Qu'ran, these are not considered to be the word of Allah, but they help Muslims understand how to live a moral life in emulation of the Prophet.

Muslims, like followers of all religions, are expected to perform certain duties. The formal acts of worship required of all Muslims are called the Five Pillars of Islam: *shahada* (the public declaration of faith), *salat* (ritual prayer performed five times daily), *zakat* (alms for the poor and needy), *sawm* (fasting during the holy month of Ramadan), and the *hajj* (pilgrimage to Mecca). Daily actions performed in obedience to Allah are also considered acts of worship. These deeds include honoring one's parents and elders, being kind to other people and animals, and always doing one's best.

The Qur'an and Sunnah gave rise to Shari'ah, or Islamic law. It has developed over time as the *'ulama'* (scholars) applied those teachings to new situations, a process of interpretation known as *itjihad*. Shari'ah is perhaps one of the most misunderstood parts of Islam in the West. Westerners usually think of *hudud*, or criminal laws, when they think of Shari'ah. However, criminal law is only a small part of Shari'ah.

The word Shari'ah literally means "path to water" or "way to a watering place." For Muslims, Shari'ah as essential for human existence: it addresses all aspects of human behavior and provides guidance on how to live an ethical and moral life.

Another aspect of Islam poorly understood by Westerners is the sectarianism within the faith. This is partly because Muslims prefer to minimize the differences among themselves when dealing with the West. The idea of unity is important to Muslims. They see themselves as part of a worldwide community of believers called the *ummah*. Yet divisions exist within Islam, just as within other religions. The two largest divisions are the Sunnis and the Shi'ah.

Almost eighty percent of Muslims today are Sunnis, whose name reflects their commitment to imitating the Sunnah. The Shi'ah split from the Sunnis in a quarrel over leadership in 661. Following Muhammad's death in 632, Muslims chose the Prophet's successors, called caliphs, to lead their community. A bitter dispute erupted following the death of the fourth caliph, 'Ali, who was Muhammad's son-in-law as well as his cousin. 'Ali's supporters—the shi'at 'Ali—insisted Islam's true leaders could come only from 'Ali's male descendants. The majority of Muslims disagreed, so 'Ali's supporters separated and became the Shi'ah. The split left lingering bad feelings between the groups. Each considers its version of Islam to be the true one and considers the other group illegitimate.

Among Sunnis, the caliph held political power but had no authority to interpret religious teachings. In Shi'ism, the leader of the community was the imam, who held religious as well as political power and was believed to be infallible.

Shi'ism itself became divided over time. One of the largest groups is the Imamis, or Twelvers, whose name comes from their focus on their twelfth imam. This twelfth imam was an infant who disappeared soon after his father, the eleventh imam, died. The Twelvers believe he went into occultation, or became hidden from view, and will return at the end of time as the *mahdi*, a figure who will establish a realm of perfection and justice. The twelfth imam's occultation left the Twelvers with no infallible authority. They turned to the *mujtahids*, the most learned *'ulama'*, to provide trustworthy interpretation of the hidden imam's will. The *mujtahids*—and particularly the leading *mujtahids* called ayatollahs—gained immense power.

Two other important movements are represented by the Sufis and the Wahhabi. Sufism, or Islamic mysticism, developed from the early reactions of some religiously sensitive Muslims against what they saw as an increasing emphasis on the external aspects of Islam. For the Sufis, it is what is inside a person that counts—"the state of the heart"—not adherence to legalist strictures.

The Wahhabi are Muslim puritans who follow the 18th-century teachings of Muhammad ibn 'Abd al-Wahhab. They call themselves al-Muwahhidun, which means "Unitarians," because they stress the absolute oneness of Allah. Unlike most Muslims, they refuse to worship saints because they feel this implies a polytheism that violates the teachings of Islam. The Wahhabi believe in a literal interpretation of the Qur'an and Hadith, and promote the foundation of an Islamic state based on Islamic law. This is the form of Islam practiced today in Saudi Arabia.

The truth about Islam bears little resemblance to the distorted image of the tradition held by many Westerners today. Islam values justice, equality, and concern for all members of society, and stresses humility and learning. These are qualities all people can appreciate, regardless of faith.

CHAPTER 1

MUHAMMAD: THE SEAL OF THE PROPHETS

The name of the Prophet Muhammad is now invoked in reverence several billion times every day. He is also the only founder of a major world religion who lived in the full light of history and about whom there are numerous records in historical texts, though, as with other premodern historical figures, the finer details of his life are unknown. The Prophet Muhammad, the founder of Islam, is one of the most influential figures in history; thus his life, deeds, and thoughts have been debated by followers and opponents over the centuries, which makes a biography of him difficult to write. At every turn both the Islamic understanding of Muhammad and the rationalist interpretation of him by Western scholars, which arose in the eighteenth and nineteenth centuries, must be considered. Moreover, on the basis of both historical evidence and the Muslim understanding of Muhammad as the Prophet, a response must be fashioned to Christian polemical writings characterizing Muhammad as an apostate, if not the Antichrist. These date back to the early Middle Ages and still influence to some degree the general Western conception of him. It is essential, therefore, both to examine the historical record—though not necessarily on the basis of secularist assumptions—and to make clear the Islamic understanding of Muhammad.

THE PROPHET'S STATURE IN THE MUSLIM COMMUNITY

The most common name of Muhammad of Islam, Muhammad ("the Glorified One"), is part of the daily call to prayer (*adhan*). Following an attestation to the oneness of God, the believer proclaims, "Verily, I bear witness that Muhammad is the Messenger of God" (*Ashhadu anna Muhammadan rasul Allah*). When this name is uttered among Muslims, it is always followed by the phrase *salla Allahu 'alayhi wa sallam* ("may God's blessings and peace be upon him").

Muhammad has many names, including "sacred names," which Muslims believe were given to him by God and by which he is called in various contexts. Traditionally, 99 names for him are commonly used in litanies and prayers. Among the most often used and also central to the understanding of his nature is Ahmad ("the Most Glorified"), which is considered an inner and celestial name for Muhammad. Over the centuries Muslim authorities have believed that when Christ spoke of the coming reign of the Paraclete, he was referring to Ahmad. Also of great importance are the names that identify Muhammad as the Prophet, including Nabi ("Prophet") and Rasul Allah ("the Messenger of God"). Other names of the Prophet are Taha ("the Pure Purifier and Guide"), Yasin ("the Perfect Man"), Mustafa ("the One Chosen"), 'Abd Allah ("the Perfect Servant of God"), Habib Allah ("the

Muhammad meets the archangel Gabriel, as depicted in the Siyer-I Nebi, *a Turkish epic written by Mustafa, son of Ysef, in 1388. The illustrations were completed in 1595.* Topkapi Palace Museum, Istanbul, Turkey/Bildarchiv Steffans/The Bridgeman Art Library

Beloved of God"), Dhikr Allah ("the Remembrance of God"), Amin ("the Trusted One"), Siraj ("the Torch Lighting the True Path"), Munir ("the Illuminator of the Universe"), Huda ("the Guide to the Truth"), Ghiyath ("the Helper"), and Ni'mat Allah ("the Gift of God"). These and his many other names play a major role in daily Muslim piety and in the practice of Sufism. An understanding of their meaning is essential to gaining any serious knowledge of the Islamic view of Muhammad or what some have called Islamic prophetology.

THE PROPHET'S LIFE

Both before the rise of Islam and during the Islamic period, Arab tribes paid great attention to genealogy and guarded their knowledge of it with meticulous care. In fact, during Islamic history a whole science of genealogy (*'ilm al-ansab*) developed that is of much historical significance. In the pre-Islamic period, however, this knowledge remained unwritten, and for that very reason it has not been taken seriously by Western historians relying only on written records. For Muslims, however, the genealogy of Muhammad has always been certain. They trace his ancestry to Isma'il (Ishmael), the son of the prophet Abraham (unlike Jews, who trace their ancestry to Abraham through Isaac).

According to traditional Islamic sources, Muhammad was born in Mecca in "the Year of the Elephant," which corresponds to the year 570 CE, the date modern Western scholars cite as at least his approximate birth date. A single event gave the Year of the Elephant its name when Abrahah, the king of Abyssinia, sent an overwhelming force to Mecca to destroy the Ka'bah, the sanctuary Muslims believe to have been built by Adam and reconstructed by Abraham and which Abrahah viewed as a

Iraqi Sunni children celebrate the birthday of Muhammad with cake and other sweets. The day of this celebration is called Mawlid an-Nabi. Khalil Al-Murshidi/AFP/Getty Images

rival to his newly constructed temple in Sanaa in Yemen. According to tradition, the elephant that marched at the head of Abrahah's army knelt as it approached Mecca, refusing to go farther. Soon the sky blackened with birds that pelted the army with pebbles, driving them off in disarray. Thus, the sanctuary that Muslims consider an earthly reflection of the celestial temple was saved, though at the time it served Arab tribes who (with the exception of the *hanifs*, or primordialists) disregarded Abrahamic monotheism.

Soon after this momentous event in the history of Arabia, Muhammad was born in Mecca. His father, 'Abd Allah, and his mother, Aminah, belonged to the family of the Banu Hashim, a branch of the powerful Quraysh, the ruling tribe of Mecca, that also guarded its most sacred shrine, the Ka'bah. Because 'Abd Allah died before Muhammad's birth, Aminah placed all her hopes in the newborn child. Without a father, Muhammad experienced many hardships even though his grandfather 'Abd al-Muttalib was a leader in the Meccan community. The emphasis in Islamic society on generosity to orphans is related to the childhood experiences of Muhammad as well as to his subsequent love for orphans and the Qur'anic injunctions concerning their treatment.

In order for Muhammad to master Arabic in its pure form and become well acquainted with Arab traditions, Aminah sent him as a baby into the desert, as was the custom of all great Arab families at that time. In the desert, it was believed, one learned the qualities of self-discipline, nobility, and freedom. A sojourn in the desert also offered escape from the domination of time and the corruption of the city. Moreover, it provided the opportunity to become a better speaker through exposure to the eloquent Arabic spoken by the Bedouin. In this way the bond with the desert and its purity and sobriety was renewed for city dwellers in every generation. Aminah chose a poor woman named Halimah from the tribe of Banu Sa'd, a branch of the Hawazin, to suckle and nurture her son. And so the young Muhammad spent several years in the desert.

It was also at this time that, according to tradition, two angels appeared to Muhammad in the guise of men, opened his breast, and purified his heart with snow. This episode exemplifies the Islamic belief that God purified his prophet and protected him from sin. Muhammad then declared, as the Hadith recounts, "Satan toucheth every son of Adam the day his mother beareth him, save only Mary and her son." Amazed by this event and also noticing a mole on Muhammad's back (the sign of prophecy according to traditional sources), Halimah and her husband, Harith, took the boy back to Mecca.

Muhammad's mother died when he was six years old. Now completely orphaned, he was brought up by his grandfather 'Abd al-Muttalib, who also died two years later. He was then placed in the care of Abu Talib, Muhammad's uncle and the father of 'Ali, Muhammad's cousin. Later in life Muhammad would repay this kindness by taking 'Ali into his household and giving his daughter Fatimah to him in marriage.

When he was 25 years old, Muhammad received a marriage proposal from a wealthy Meccan woman, Khadijah bint al-Khuwaylid, whose affairs he was conducting. Despite the fact that she was 15 years older than he, Muhammad accepted the proposal, and he did not take another wife until after her death (though polygyny was permitted and common). She bore him two sons, both of whom died young. It is from the first son, Qasim, that one of the names of the Prophet, Abu' al-Qasim ("the Father of Qasim"), derives. She also bore him four daughters, Zaynab, Ruqayyah, Umm Kulthum, and Fatimah. The youngest, Fatimah, who is called the second Mary, had the greatest impact on history of all his children. Shi'ite imams and sayyids or sharifs are thought to be descendants of Muhammad, from the lineage of Fatimah and 'Ali.

By age 35, Muhammad had become a very respected figure in Mecca and had taken 'Ali into his household. According to the traditional account, when he was asked to arbitrate a dispute concerning which tribe should place the holy black stone in the corner of the newly built Ka'bah (an altar in Mecca that subsequently became the holiest shrine of Islam), Muhammad resolved the conflict by putting his cloak on the ground with the stone in the middle and having a representative of each tribe lift a corner of it until the stone reached the appropriate height to be set in the wall. His reputation stemmed, in part, from his deep religiosity and attention to prayer. He often would leave the city and retire to the desert for prayer and meditation. Moreover, before the advent of his prophecy, he received visions that he described as being like "the breaking of the light of dawn." It was during one of these periods of retreat, when he was 40 years old and meditating in a cave called al-Hira' in the Mountain of Light (Jabal al-Nur) near Mecca, that the process of the Qur'anic revelation began.

In the month of Ramadan in the year 610, according to Islamic tradition, the archangel Gabriel appeared to Muhammad in the form of a man, asked him to "recite" (*iqra'*), and then overwhelmed him with a very strong embrace. Muhammad told the stranger that he was not a reciter and was, in fact, unlettered (*ummi*). But the angel repeated his demand and embrace three times, after which the verses of the Qur'an, beginning with "Recite in the Name of thy Lord who created," were revealed. Muhammad fled the cave thinking that he had become possessed by the *jinn*, or demons. When he heard a voice saying, "Thou art the messenger of God and I am Gabriel," Muhammad ran down the mountain. Gazing upward, he saw the man who had spoken to him in his real form, an angel so immense that in whatever direction the Prophet looked the celestial figure covered the sky, which had turned green (thereafter the colour of Islam). Muhammad returned home, and, when the effect of the great awe in his soul abated, he told Khadijah what had happened. She believed his account and sent for her blind cousin Waraqah, a Christian who possessed much religious wisdom. Having heard the account, Waraqah confirmed what Gabriel had told him: Muhammad had been chosen as God's prophet. Shortly thereafter, Muhammad received a second revelation. As the Prophet later said, the revelation would either come through the words of the archangel or be directly revealed to him in his heart. The revelation was also accompanied by the sound of bell-like reverberations. According to Islamic tradition, this was the beginning of a process of the revelation of the Qur'an that lasted some 23 years and ended shortly before the Prophet's death.

Muhammad first preached his message to the members of his family, then to a few friends, and finally, three years after the advent of the revelation, to the public at large. The first to accept Muhammad's call to become Muslims after Khadijah were 'Ali; Zayd ibn al-Harith, who was like a son to the Prophet; and Abu Bakr, a venerable member of the Meccan community who was the Prophet's close friend. This small group was the centre from which Islam grew in ever-wider circles. A number of prominent Meccans also embraced Islam. Yet most influential figures and families, especially those prominent in trade, rejected his call. Even within his family there were skeptics. Although Muhammad gained the support of many of the Banu Hashim, his uncle Abu Lahab, a major leader of the Quraysh (the Arabic tribe to which the Prophet belonged), remained adamantly opposed to Islam and Muhammad's mission. These naysayers feared that the new religion, based on the oneness of God and unequivocally opposed to idolatry, would destroy the favoured position of the Ka'bah as the centre of the religious cults of various Arab tribes and hence jeopardize the commerce that accompanied the pilgrimage to Mecca to worship idols kept there.

Meanwhile, life for Muhammad and the early Muslims was becoming ever more difficult and dangerous as the result of extreme pressure exerted upon them by the Quraysh rulers of the city. Even the conversions of leaders of the Meccan community, such as 'Umar al-Khattab and 'Uthman ibn 'Affan, did not diminish the severe difficulties encountered by Muhammad in his later years in Mecca.

Moreover, Muhammad was soon greatly saddened by the death of two people who were especially close to him. Khadijah, not only his devoted wife of 25 years and the mother of his children but also his friend and counselor, died in 619. Only after her death did Muhammad marry other women, mostly as a means of creating alliances with various families and tribes. The exception was the daughter of Abu Bakr, 'A'ishah, who was betrothed to the Prophet when she was very young and in whose arms he would die in Medina. Later in the year, Abu Talib, Muhammad's uncle and protector, died, creating a much more difficult situation for him and for the young Islamic community in Mecca. These deaths, combined with Muhammad's lack of success in propagating the message of Islam in the city of Ta'if, severely tested his determination and resolve.

As if by heavenly compensation, during this extremely difficult time Muhammad underwent the supreme spiritual experience of his life. On one of his nightly visits to the Ka'bah, he fell asleep in the Hijr, an uncovered sanctuary attached to the north wall of the Ka'bah, and experienced the Nocturnal Ascent (Isra' or Mi'raj). This event has become the subject of countless later mystical and philosophical writings. According to traditional accounts, among which there are certain minor variations, Muhammad was taken by Gabriel on the winged steed Buraq to Jerusalem. From the rock upon which Abraham offered to sacrifice his son (now the site of the Dome of the Rock, one of Islam's earliest and greatest mosques), they ascended through all the higher states of being to the Divine Presence itself. At one point Gabriel explained that he could go no farther because, were he to do so, his wings would be burned. But Muhammad, according to the Qur'an, reached a state higher than that of the archangels. Ascending through higher states of being symbolized by the heavenly spheres, Muhammad not only met such earlier great prophets as Moses and Jesus, but he received the supreme treasury of knowledge while he stood and then prostrated himself before the divine throne. God also revealed to him the final form and number of the Islamic daily prayers.

The Mi'raj reconstituted Muhammad's resolve. Despite the setback in Ta'if, the vision of spreading the message of Islam beyond Mecca grew in his mind. In or around 621 a delegation from Yathrib, a city north of Mecca, contacted Muhammad and, having heard of his sense of justice and power of leadership, invited him to go to their city and become their leader. At that time Yathrib suffered from constant struggle between its two leading tribes, the 'Aws and the Khazraj, with a sizable Jewish community constituting the third important social group of the city. After some deliberation by Muhammad, a preliminary meeting was held in Al-'Aqabah (in present-day Jordan), and the next year a formal agreement was made with the people of Yathrib according to which Muhammad and his followers would be protected by the people of that city. Upon finalizing the agreement, Muhammad ordered his followers to leave Mecca in small groups, so as not to attract attention, and to await him in Yathrib.

Finally, he departed one evening with Abu Bakr for Yathrib, using an indirect route after commanding 'Ali to sleep in the Prophet's bed. The Quraysh, who had decided

MI'RAJ

Traditional Muslims believe that the Mi'raj, the ascension of the Prophet Muhammad into heaven, was not only spiritual but also corporeal in the same way that, according to traditional Christian belief, Christ's Ascension was accomplished in both body and spirit. According to tradition, Muhammad is prepared for his meeting with God by the archangels Gabriel and Michael one evening while he is asleep in the Ka'bah, the sacred shrine of Mecca. They open up his body and purify his heart by removing all traces of error, doubt, idolatry, and paganism and by filling it with wisdom and belief. In the original version of the Mi'raj, the Prophet is then transported by Gabriel directly to the lowest heaven. But early in Muslim history the story of the ascension came to be associated with the story of Muhammad's night journey (Isra') from the "sacred place of worship" (Mecca) to the "further place of worship" (Jerusalem). The two separate incidents were gradually combined so that chronologically the purification of Muhammad in his sleep begins the sequence; he is then transported in a single night from Mecca to Jerusalem by the winged mythical creature Buraq, and from Jerusalem he ascends to heaven, possibly by ladder (*mi'raj*), accompanied by Gabriel.

Muhammad and Gabriel enter the first heaven and proceed through all seven levels until they reach the throne of God. Along the way they meet the prophets Adam, John, Jesus, Joseph, Idris, Aaron, Moses, and Abraham and visit hell and paradise. Moses alone of all the inhabitants of heaven speaks at any length to the visitors. He says that Muhammad is more highly regarded by God than himself and that Muhammad's following outnumbers his own. Once Muhammad appears before God, he is told to recite the *salat* (ritual prayer) 50 times each day. Moses, however, advises Muhammad to plead for a reduction of the number as being too difficult for believers, and the obligation is eventually reduced to five prayers each day.

The Mi'raj is the prototype of spiritual realization in Islam and signifies the final integration of the spiritual, psychic, and physical elements of the human state. Parallels have been drawn between the Mi'raj and the manner in which a dead man's soul will progress to judgment at God's throne; the Sufis (Muslim mystics) claim it describes the soul's leap into mystic knowledge. Popularly the ascension is celebrated with readings of the legend on the 27th day of Rajab, called *Laylat al-Mi'raj* ("Night of the Ascension").

to get rid of the Prophet once and for all, attacked the house but found 'Ali in his place. They then set out to find the Prophet. According to the traditional story, Muhammad and Abu Bakr hid in a cave that was then camouflaged by spiders, which spun webs over its mouth, and birds, which placed their nests in front of the cave. Once the search party arrived at the mouth of the cave, they decided not to go in because the unbroken cobwebs and undisturbed nests seemed to indicate that no one could be inside.

On Sept. 25, 622, Muhammad completed the Hijrah ("migration"; Latin: Hegira) and reached Yathrib, which became known as Madinat al-Nabi ("City of the Prophet"), or Medina. This momentous event led to the establishment of Islam as a religious and social order and became the starting point for the Islamic calendar. The caliph 'Umar I, who was one of the successors of Muhammad as the leader of Islam, was the first to use this dating system and established the first day of the lunar month of Muharram, which corresponds to July 16, 622, as the beginning of the Islamic calendar. Muhammad arrived in Quba', on the outskirts of Medina, where he ordered the first mosque of Islam to be built. The people of the city came in large numbers to greet him, and each family wanted to take him to its own quarters. Therefore, he said that his camel, Qaswra', should be allowed to go where it willed, and where it stopped, he would stay. A mosque, known later as the Mosque of the Prophet (Masjid al-Nabi), was built in the courtyard next to the house where the camel stopped and Muhammad lived. Muhammad's tomb is in the mosque.

When Muhammad first settled in Medina, his most trusted followers were those who had migrated from Mecca. Soon, however, many Medinans embraced Islam, so the early Islamic community came to consist of the emigrants (al-muhajirun) and the Medinan helpers (al-ansar). A few Medinan families and such prominent figures as 'Abd Allah ibn Ubayy held back, but gradually all the Arabs of Medina embraced Islam. Nevertheless, tribal divisions remained, along with a continued Jewish presence that included wealthy tribes that enjoyed the support of Jewish communities farther north, especially in Khaybar. Muhammad hoped that they would embrace Islam and accept him as a prophet, but that happened in only a few cases. On the contrary, as Muhammad integrated the Medinan community—the muhajirun and the ansar and the 'Aws and Khazraj tribes—into an Islamic society, the enmity between Medina's Jewish community and the newly founded Islamic order grew.

During the second year of the Hijrah, Muhammad drew up the Constitution of Medina, defining relations between the various groups in the first Islamic community. Later generations of Islamic political thinkers have paid much attention to the constitution, for Muslims believe that Muhammad created the ideal Islamic society in Medina, providing a model for all later generations. It was a society in which the integration of tribal groups and various social and economic classes was based on social justice. According to Islamic belief, that same year the direction

HIJRAH

The Prophet Muhammad's migration (622 CE) from Mecca to Medina in order to escape persecution is the starting point of the Muslim calendar. The term *hijrah* has also been applied to the immigrations of the faithful to Ethiopia and of Muhammad's followers to Medina before the capture of Mecca. Muslims who later quitted lands under Christian rule were also called *muhajirun* ("emigrants").

The most honoured *muhajirun*, considered among those known as the Companions of the Prophet, are those who immigrated with Muhammad to Medina. Muhammad praised them highly for having forsaken their native city and following him and promised that God would favour them. They remained a separate and greatly esteemed group in the Muslim community, both in Mecca and in Medina, and assumed leadership of the Muslim state, through the caliphate, after Muhammad's death.

As a result of the Hijrah, another distinct body of Muslims had come into being, the *ansar* ("helpers"). The *ansar* were members of the two major Medinese tribes, the feuding al-Khazraj and al-Aws, whom Muhammad had been asked to reconcile when he was still a rising figure in Mecca. They came to be his devoted supporters, constituting three-fourths of the Muslim army at the Battle of Badr , which would be fought in 624. When no one of their number was chosen to the caliphate to succeed Muhammad, they declined in influence as a group and eventually merged with other Muslims who had settled in Medina.

In 639 'Umar I, the second caliph, introduced a dating system from the Hijrah era (now distinguished by the initials AH, for Latin *Anno Hegirae*, "in the year of the Hijrah"). 'Umar started the first year AH with the first day of the lunar month of Muharram, which corresponded to July 16, 622. In 1677–78 (AH 1088) the Ottoman government, still keeping the Hijrah era, began to use the solar year of the Julian calendar, eventually creating two different Hijrah era dates, resulting from the differences between a solar and lunar year.

of daily prayers, or the *qiblah*, was changed by divine order from Jerusalem to Mecca. Jerusalem has, however, continued to be revered as the first direction of the prayers chosen by God for Muslims, and, according to Islamic eschatological teachings, the first *qiblah* will become one with the *qiblah* at Mecca at the end of time.

Later in 623 the message of Islam was explicitly defined as a return to the primordial monotheism (*al-din al-hanif*) of Abraham. While some Western scholars have called the second year of the Hijrah the period of the establishment of a theocracy led by Muhammad, the Islamic community at Medina in fact established a nomocracy under Divine Law, with Muhammad as the executor. Until his death, Muhammad not only continued to be the channel for the revelation of the Qur'an but also ruled the community of Muslims. He was also the supreme interpreter of the law of Medinan society.

The enmity between the Quraysh and Muhammad remained very strong, in part because of the persecution, aggression, and confiscation of property the Muslims suffered at the hands of the Quraysh. On several occasions warriors from Medina intercepted caravans from Mecca going to or coming from Syria, but Muhammad did not want to fight a battle against the Meccans until they marched against the nascent Medinan community and threatened the very future of Islam. At this time the following Qur'anic verse was revealed: "Permission to fight is granted to those against whom war is made, because they have been wronged, and God indeed has the power to help them. They are those who have been driven out of their homes unjustly only because they affirmed: Our Lord is God" (sura 22, verses 39–40). Muslims viewed this revelation as a declaration of war by God against the idolatrous Quraysh. In 624 an army of 1,000 assembled by the

Quraysh marched against Medina and met a much smaller force of 313 Muslims at a place called Badr on the 17th day of the month of Ramadan. Muslims view this event as the most momentous battle of Islamic history, and many later crucial battles were named after it. Muhammad promised all those who were killed at Badr the death of a martyr and direct entry into paradise. Although heavily outnumbered, the Muslims achieved a remarkable victory in which, however, nine of the Companions of the Prophet (*al-sahabah*), the close associates of Muhammad and the faithful who were associated directly with him, were killed. Muslims believe that the battle was won with the help of the angels, and to this day the whole episode remains etched deeply in the historical consciousness of Muslims.

The Quraysh did not give up their quest to destroy the nascent Islamic community. In 624–625 they dispatched an army of 3,000 men under the leader of Mecca, Abu Sufyan. Muhammad led his forces to the side of a mountain near Medina called Uhud, and battle ensued. The Muslims had some success early in the engagement, but Khalid ibn al-Walid, a leading Meccan general and later one of the outstanding military figures of early Islamic history, charged Muhammad's left flank after the Muslims on guard deserted their posts to join in the looting of the Quraysh camp. Many of Muhammad's followers then fled, thinking that the Prophet had fallen (although wounded, he was led to safety through a ravine). Meanwhile, the Quraysh did not pursue their victory. A number of eminent Muslims, including Muhammad's valiant uncle Hamzah, however, lost their lives in the struggle. The Jews of Medina, who were alleged to have plotted with the Quraysh, rejoiced in Muhammad's defeat, and one of their tribes, the Banu Nadir, was therefore seized and banished by Muhammad to Khaybar.

The Jews of Medina then urged the Quraysh to take over Medina in 626–627. The Quraysh helped raise a 10,000-man army, which marched on Medina. Salman al-Farsi, the first Persian convert to Islam whom Muhammad had adopted as a member of his household, suggested that the Muslims dig a ditch around the city to protect it, a technique known to the Persians but not to the Arabs at that time. The Meccan army arrived and, unable to cross the ditch, laid siege to the city but without success. The invading army gradually began to disperse, leaving the Muslims victorious in the Battle of the Ditch (*al-Khandaq*).

When it was discovered that members of the Jewish tribe Qurayzah had been complicit with the enemy during the Battle of the Ditch, Muhammad turned against them. The Qurayzah men were separated from the tribe's women and children and ordered by the Muslim general Sa'd ibn Mu'adh to be put to death; the women and children were to be enslaved. This tragic episode cast a shadow upon the relations between the two communities for many centuries, even though the Jews, a "People of the Book" (that is, like Christians and Zoroastrians, as well as Muslims, possessors of a divinely revealed scripture), generally enjoyed the protection of their lives, property, and religion under Islamic rule and fared better in the Muslim world than in the West. Moreover, Muslims believe that the Prophet did not order the execution of the Jews of Medina. Many Western historians, however, believe that he must have been informed of it.

The Islamic community had become more solidly established by 628, when Muhammad decided to make the *'umrah* ("lesser pilgrimage") to the Ka'bah. He set out for Mecca with a large entourage and many animals meant for sacrifice, but an armed Meccan contingent blocked his way. Because he had intended to perform a religious rite, he did not want to battle the Meccans at that time. So he camped at a site known as Al-Hudaybiyah and sent 'Uthman to Mecca to negotiate a peaceful visit. When 'Uthman was delayed, Muhammad assembled his followers and had them make a pact of allegiance (al-bay'ah) to follow him under all conditions unto death. 'Uthman finally returned with Quraysh leaders who proposed as a compromise that Muhammad return to Medina but make a peaceful pilgrimage to Mecca the next year. In addition, a 10-year truce was signed with the Meccans.

Muhammad's first conquest was made in 628–629 when the Muslims captured Khaybar in a battle in which the valour of 'Ali played an important role. The Jews and Christians of Khaybar were allowed to live in peace, protected by the Muslims, but they were required to pay a religious tax called the *jizyah*. This arrangement, under which non-Muslims were accorded *dhimmah* ("protected") status, became the model for the later treatment of People of the Book in Islamic history. It was also at this time that Muhammad, according to Islamic sources, sent letters inviting various leaders to accept Islam, including Muqawqis, the governor of Alexandria; the negus of Abyssinia; Heraclius, the emperor of Byzantium; and Khosrow II, the king of Persia. In these letters he emphasized that there should be no compulsion for People of the Book—Jews, Christians, or Zoroastrians—to accept Islam.

During this time, Muhammad finally made a pilgrimage to Mecca, where he reconciled with members of his family and also many of his followers. A number of eminent Meccans—including two later major military and political figures, Khalid ibn al-Walid and 'Amr ibn al-'As— accepted Islam. Meanwhile, Islam continued to spread throughout Arabia, as many northern tribes embraced Islam. Shortly thereafter, however, the Quraysh broke the pact agreed upon at Al-Hudaybiyah, freeing Muhammad to march on Mecca, which he did with a large group of the *ansar*, the *muhajirun*, and Bedouins. The Quraysh plea for amnesty was granted. After many years of hardship and exile, Muhammad entered Mecca triumphantly, directing his followers not to take revenge for the persecution many of them had endured. He went directly to the Ka'bah, where he ordered 'Ali and Bilal, the Abyssinian caller to prayer (*al-mu'adhdhin*), to remove all the idols and restore the Ka'bah to the purity it had enjoyed when Abraham had reconsecrated it as the house of the one God. All the Meccans then embraced Islam.

Although the Islamization of Arabia was not yet complete, embassies from all over the Arabian Peninsula arrived in Medina to accept Islam. By 630–631 most of Arabia, save for the north, had united under the religion's banner. Muhammad, therefore, marched with a large army north to Tabuk but did not engage the enemy. Nevertheless, the Jews and Christians of the region submitted to his authority, and Muhammad guaranteed their personal safety and freedom to practice their religion as he did for the Zoroastrians of eastern Arabia. At that time too the pagan Arab tribes in the north, as well as in other regions, embraced Islam. By 631 Muhammad had brought to a close "the age of ignorance" (*al-jahiliyyah*), as Muslims called the pre-Islamic epoch in Arabia, and united the Arabs for the first time in history under the banner of Islam. Tribal relations were not fully destroyed, but they were now transcended by a more powerful bond based on religion.

Finally, in 632, Muhammad made the first Islamic pilgrimage to Mecca (*al-hajj*). This event, which remains the model to this day for the millions of Muslims who make the *hajj* each year, marked the peak of Muhammad's earthly life. At that time he delivered his celebrated farewell sermon, and the last verse of the Qur'an, completing the sacred text, was revealed: "This day have I perfected for you your religion and fulfilled My favour unto you, and it hath been My good pleasure to choose Islam for you as your religion" (sura 5, verse 3). On the way back from Mecca, he and his entourage stopped at a pond called Ghadir Khumm where, according to both Sunni and Shi'ite sources, he appointed 'Ali as the executor of his last will and as his *wali,* a term that means "friend" or "saint" and also describes a person who possesses authority. Sunni Muslims interpret this major event as signifying a personal and family matter, while Shi'ites believe that at this time 'Ali received the formal investiture to succeed the Prophet.

Late in the spring of 632, Muhammad suddenly fell ill and, according to tradition, died three days later on June 8. His legacy included the establishment of a new order that would transform and affect much of the world from the Atlantic to the Pacific. According to Islamic norms that he established, his body was washed by his family, especially by 'Ali, and buried in his house adjacent to the mosque of Medina. His tomb, visited annually by millions of pilgrims, remains the holiest place in Islam after the Ka'bah.

CHAPTER 2

GOD'S WORD
TO HUMANITY

There is something of the soul of the Prophet Muhammad in the Qur'an, the holy book of Islam that tradition holds was originally a sonorous revelation from God imprinted upon the Prophet's heart and only later written down. If the text of the Qur'an is comparable to words heard by the ear, the soul of the Prophet is like the air that carries the sound and allows it to be heard by humanity. According to a famous saying from him (known as *hadith al-thaqalayn*), Muhammad said that, when he departed from the world, he would leave behind two precious gifts (*thaqalayn*): the Qur'an and his family. When asked by his wife 'A'ishah how he should be remembered after his death, Muhammad replied, "By reciting the Qur'an." The very subtle relationship between the Qur'an and the Prophet causes Muslims to feel his grace (*barakah*) whenever they read the Qur'an, which they nevertheless understand to be the pronouncement to humanity of the Word of God revealed through the agency of the archangel Gabriel to Muhammad, a pious but unlettered person, and uttered verbatim by him to those around him.

THE QUR'AN

The Qur'an is the central theophany (divine manifestation) of Islam. Although most modern Muslims know it as the Holy Qur'an, many of them still refer to it as *al-Qur'an al-karim* or *al-Qur'an al-majid*, which can best be translated as "the Noble Qur'an" or "the Glorious Qur'an." Composed in Arabic, Islam's sacred liturgical language, the Qur'an is untranslatable. The name Qur'an is derived from the term *al-qur'an*, meaning "the recitation." The scripture has many other names, each of which suggests an aspect of its significance for Muslims. Among those found in the text itself are *al-furqan* ("discernment"), *umm al-kitab* (the "mother book," or "archetypal

A man reads from the Qur'an in the Sanaa Grand Mosque in Yemen. The Qur'an did not exist in book form until after Muhammad's death. Khaled Fazaa/AFP/Getty Images

book"), *al-huda* ("the guide"), *dhikrallah* ("the remembrance of God"), *al-hikmah* ("wisdom"), and *kalamallah* ("the Word of God").

Traditional Muslims believe that the Qur'an exists eternally with God in the Guarded Tablet (*al-lawh al-mahfaz*)—a tablet in the spiritual world on which the text of the Qur'an was inscribed before its descent into this world—as God's Word and that through the divine will the book was revealed to the Prophet word for word and sentence by sentence through the agency of the archangel Gabriel. Muhammad received his first revelation in the cave of Hira near Mecca in 610 and continued receiving revelations until 629. Muslims believe that the illiterate Muhammad did not alter the revelations by a single word.

The Qur'an asserts that Muhammad was a man and not a divine being, that he was the "seal of prophets" (*khatam al-anbiya*'), that he was endowed with the most exalted character, and that God had placed him as the "goodly model" (*uswah hasanah*) for Muslims to follow. Islamic tradition thus considers Muhammad to be the person who best comprehended the meaning of the Qur'an and was its first interpreter and commentator. Over the centuries all traditional Muslims have understood the Qur'an through Muhammad's interpretation, and whenever they recite the Qur'an or seek to put its teachings into practice, they experience his presence. Islamic sages over the ages, in fact, have insisted that God granted to the Prophet alone the understanding of all levels of the Qur'an's meaning that humans could grasp and that those who later came to know something of the inner meaning of the Qur'an were heirs to the knowledge given to Muhammad by God.

The Qur'an has long been considered the supreme standard of eloquence in the Arabic language. Qur'anic Arabic has been studied by non-Arab Muslims all over the world because the daily prayer recited by all Muslims consists primarily of Qur'anic verses in Arabic. Muslims believe that the Arabic language of the Qur'an is indispensable in conveying God's message because it was chosen by God himself. In the same way that everything concerning Christ is sacred for Christians, everything concerning the Qur'an is sacred for Muslims. In keeping with the verse, "None toucheth [the Qur'an] save the purified" (sura 56, verse 79), most Muslims perform ritual ablutions before touching the Qur'an, which is always found in a place of honour in the home or the mosque.

The text of the Qur'an seems outwardly to have no beginning, middle, or end; its nonlinear structure is like that of a web or a net. It consists of 114 chapters called suras, a term mentioned several times and identified as units or chapters of the revelation. The title of each sura is derived from a name or quality discussed in the text or from the first letters or words of the sura. Muslims believe that the Prophet himself, on God's command, gave the suras their names. The opening chapter, Al-Fatihah (The Opening), is the heart of the Qur'an and is repeated in daily prayers and on many other occasions. The second sura, Al-Baqarah (The Cow), is the longest, and subsequent chapters are arranged according to length, with chapters becoming shorter as the text proceeds. All suras except one, Al-Tawba (Repentance), begin with the formula *Bismi'llah al-Rahman al-Rahim* ("In the Name of God, the Infinitely Good, the All Merciful"), which is the formula pious Muslims use whenever they consecrate something. The suras are further subdivided between those that were revealed to Muhammad in Mecca and those that were revealed to him in Medina. According to traditional Islamic authorities, the ordering of the chapters was also revealed to the Prophet and is not an ad hoc arrangement made by later scribes, as is claimed by many Western scholars, who do not accept the revealed nature of the Qur'an.

Each sura is divided into verses called *ayahs*, from a term originally meaning a sign or portent sent by God to reveal an aspect of his wisdom. The number of *ayahs* in each sura ranges from three or four to more than 200, and an individual *ayah* may be as brief as one or two words or as long as several lines. The verses of the Qur'an, however, should not be understood as poetry in the ordinary sense. Although the Qur'an is extremely poetical, its *ayahs* are unlike the highly refined poetry of the pre-Islamic Arabs in their content and distinctive rhymes and rhythms, being more akin to the prophetic utterances marked by inspired discontinuities found in the sacred scriptures of Judaism and Christianity.

Since the beginning of Islam, the proper number of *ayahs* has been a topic of dispute among Muslim scholars, some recognizing 6,000, some 6,204, some 6,219, and some 6,236, although the words in all cases are the same. Indeed, the study of the enumeration of the verses of the Qur'an developed very early in Islamic history at the schools of Mecca, Kufa, Basra, and Sham. The most popular edition of the Qur'an, which is based on the tradition of the school of Kufa, contains 6,236 *ayahs*.

Complementing the organization into suras and *ayahs*, there is a crosscutting division into 30 parts, *juz's*, each containing two units called *hizbs*, each of which in turn is divided into four parts (*rub 'al-ahzabs*). These divisions facilitate the reading of the Qur'an over periods of different lengths. For example, since Muslims believe that the Qur'an was first revealed during the holy month of Ramadan, a time of prayer and fasting, many people recite one *juz'* each day and therefore complete the reading of the Qur'an during the month. The Qur'an is also divided into seven stations, or *manazils*, for those who wish to recite the whole text during one week.

As Muhammad first heard the Qur'an before uttering it and writing it down, so do the great majority of modern Muslims experience it through recitation. Most Muslims are not Arabs and do not know Arabic, and among Arabs a large number are not literate. Nevertheless, throughout the Islamic world the Qur'an is present on nearly every occasion through its being chanted according to traditional norms dating to the origin of the religion, its chanting constituting one of the sacred Islamic arts. A Muslim who knows the Qur'an by heart, of whom there are many, is called a *hafiz*, which means "one who has memorized the sacred text."

As the sacred scripture of a world religion, the Qur'an contains all the guidance necessary for Muslims, and there is practically no aspect of life with which it does not deal. Above all, the Qur'an is concerned with the ultimate nature of reality, or God (Allah); Muslims believe that the Qur'an's exposition of this reality is the most complete possible. The Qur'an emphasizes the oneness of God, or the doctrine of *tawhid*, in verses such as "Allah, there is no god but Him" (sura 2, verse 255–sura 3, verse 2). God is both completely transcendent and completely imminent; his closeness to humans is asserted in the verse proclaiming that God is closer to humans "than one's own jugular vein" (sura 50, verse 6). To Muslims, religion is inseparable from human existence, and indeed it is ingrained in humanity's primordial nature (*al-fitrah*).

One of the major themes of the Qur'an is the meaning of ethical action and the battle between good and evil. All human actions have consequences for the soul beyond its earthly life, and therefore discussion of good and evil is inseparable from the consideration of eschatology, or the doctrine of the endtimes. The Qur'an asserts a direct relation between God and humans, without any priestly intermediary; each man and woman is seen as God's "vice-gerent" on Earth. Despite this direct relationship, humans are portrayed as forgetful beings and are therefore commanded to obey God's laws. Submission to God's will is of primary importance—the name of the religion, *al-islam*, is derived from the root *slm*, meaning "surrender" or "peace." Men and women are expected to be virtuous, to pray, and to perform their duties to family, to society, and indeed to creation as a whole.

The Qur'an contains specific laws and legal principles for governing Islamic society, such as laws of inheritance. Islamic law in its systematized form is known as Shari'ah. Rights are treated as secondary to the individual's obligations to God and to creation. Throughout the Qur'an a balance is created between the rights and obligations of the individual and the community, in light of God's laws and commandments, as well as between man's duties toward God and his duties toward society and the world of nature. For example, human beings are given freedom by God, and they are obligated to pray to God. They have the right to own property but not what is of a public nature. Society must in turn protect the property of its members. Human beings can also make use of various creatures in nature but must also protect animals and plants and not squander natural resources.

The Qur'an asserts that belief in the unity of God is at the heart of all authentic religions, and it uses the singular rather than the plural when referring to religion. At the same time, it states explicitly that there are no people to whom God has not sent a messenger, and it mentions some of the prophets of Judaism and Christianity by name. The Qur'an presents a universal perspective on religion, maintaining that all revealed books are contained in the *umm al-kitab* ("archetypal book"). According to the Qur'an, there is oneness of the truth, but there is also diversity in religions because of the diversity of humanity. Muslims, therefore, are asked to accept the Torah, the Gospels, and other books; further, Muslims also must respect the followers of other religions, such as Zoroastrianism, Judaism, and Christianity (which the Qur'an considers to be the "People of the Book," Ahl al-Kitab) and must recognize that there are virtuous people in other religious communities. The idea of the People of the Book was applied later by Muslims in India to Hinduism and in some cases to Buddhism and in China to Confucianism. The Qur'an invites followers of different religions to meet on the basis of the oneness of God (sura 3, verse 64). Although it rejects the divinity of Christ—whose miraculous birth and exalted position among prophets it nevertheless confirms explicitly—it asserts that, among all other religions, the one closest to Islam is Christianity.

It is difficult to exaggerate the importance of the Qur'an in the life of Muslims. Verses of the Qur'an are recited to Muslims at birth, the psalmody of the text surrounds them at the time of death, and, at all points in between, their lives are imbued with its presence. Those who can read the text do so regularly, and others listen to it constantly. For each Muslim the Qur'an is like a person with whom he or she becomes more intimate as he or she grows older. The verses of the Qur'an are thought to have power over body and soul, healing both. The sense of the protective power of the Qur'an is so great that many Muslims carry small copies of it with them almost always. Many Islamic cities had—and a few still have—a copy of the Qur'an at the top of their gates, so that travelers who enter will receive the blessing of its protection.

Despite the diversity of the Islamic world, belief in the sacredness of the Qur'an in all of its aspects—from the sound of its recitation to the paper upon which it is written—is universal. All Muslims recite the Qur'an in a state of reverence, usually while facing their *qiblah*—that is, the direction of the Ka'bah. The Qur'an is the foundation of Islam as a world religion and the basis upon which Islamic civilization was created. It is also for Muslims the ultimate link between the individual and God, a net cast by God into the world in order to ensnare the wandering soul and bring it back to Allah, the One, who is the beginning and end of all things.

NO GOD BUT GOD: ALLAH

Islam holds that Allah is the one and only God. Etymologically, his name is probably a contraction of the Arabic *al-Ilah*, "the God." The name's origin can be traced back to the earliest Semitic writings in which the word for "god" was *Il* or *El*, the latter being a synonym for *Yahweh* in the Hebrew Bible. Allah is the standard Arabic word for "God" and is also used by Arab Christians as well as by Muslims. Allah is the pivot of the Muslim faith. The Qur'an constantly preaches Allah's reality, his inaccessible mystery, and his actions on behalf of his creatures. Three themes preponderate: (1) Allah is the Creator, Judge, and Rewarder; (2) he is unique (*wahid*) and inherently one (*ahad*); and (3) he is omnipotent and all-merciful. Allah is the "Lord of the Worlds," the Most High; "nothing is like unto him," and this in itself is to the believer a request to adore Allah as the Protector and to glorify his powers of compassion and forgiveness. The Qur'an proclaims that Allah "loves those who do good" and expresses a mutual love between him and humanity, but the Judeo-Christian precept to "love God with all thy heart" is nowhere formulated in Islam. The emphasis is rather on Allah's inscrutable sovereignty, to which one must abandon oneself. In essence, the "surrender to Allah" (*islam*) is the religion itself.

Muslim piety has collected, in the Qur'an and in the Hadith (the sayings of the Prophet Muhammad), the 99 "most beautiful names" (*al-asma' al-husna*) of Allah. These names have become objects of devoted recitation and meditation. Among the names of Allah are the One and Only, the Living One, the Subsisting (*al-Hayy al-Qayyum*), the Real Truth (*al-Haqq*), the Sublime (*al-'Azim*), the Wise (*al-Hakim*), the Omnipotent (*al-'Aziz*), the Hearer (*al-Sami'*), the Seer (*al-Basir*), the Omniscient (*al-'Alim*), the Witness (*al-Shahid*), the Trustee (*al-Wakil*), the Benefactor (*al-Rahman*), the Merciful (*al-Rahim*), and the Constant Forgiver (*al-Ghafur, al-Ghaffar*).

At all times there have been freethinkers in Islam, but rare has been the Muslim thinker who has denied the very existence of Allah. Indeed, the profession of faith (*shaha-dah*) by which a person is introduced into the Muslim community consists of the affirmation that there is no god but Allah and that Muhammad is his prophet. For pious Muslims, every action is opened by an invocation of the divine name (*basmalah*). The formula *insha'a Allah,* "if Allah wills," appears frequently in daily speech. This formula is the reminder of an ever-present divine intervention in the order of the world and the actions of human beings. Muslims believe that nothing happens and nothing is performed unless it is by the will or commandment of Allah. The personal attitude of a Muslim believer, therefore, is a complete submission to Allah, "whom one does not question" but whom one knows according to his (Qur'anic) word to be a fair judge, at once formidable, benevolent, and the Supreme Help.

The doctrine about God in the Qur'an is rigorously monotheistic: God is one and unique; he has no partner and no equal. Trinitarianism, the Christian belief that God is three persons in one substance, is vigorously repudiated. Muslims believe that there are no intermediaries between

TAWHID

Islam proclaims the oneness of God in the sense that he is one and there is no god but him, as stated in the *shahadah*, the profession of faith: "There is no god but God, and Muhammad is His prophet." *Tawhid* is the doctrine of the unity of God, and the issues that it raises—such as the question of the relation between the essence and the attributes of God—reappear throughout most of Islamic history. In the terminology of Muslim mystics (Sufis), however, *tawhid* means that all essences are divine, and there is no absolute existence beside that of God. To most Muslim scholars, the science of *tawhid* is the systematic theology through which a better knowledge of God may be reached; to the Sufis, knowledge of God can be reached only through religious experience and direct vision.

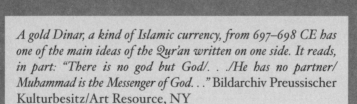

A gold Dinar, a kind of Islamic currency, from 697–698 CE has one of the main ideas of the Qur'an written on one side. It reads, in part: "There is no god but God/. . ./He has no partner/ Muhammad is the Messenger of God. . ." Bildarchiv Preussischer Kulturbesitz/Art Resource, NY

God and the creation that he brought into being. Although his presence is believed to be everywhere, he is not incarnated in anything. He is the sole creator and sustainer of the universe, wherein every creature bears witness to his unity and lordship. But he is also just and merciful: his justice ensures order in his creation, in which nothing is believed to be out of place, and his mercy is unbounded and encompasses everything. His creation and ordering of the universe is viewed as the act of prime mercy for which all things sing his glories. The God of the Qur'an, described as majestic and sovereign, is also a personal God who responds whenever a person is in distress. Above all, he is the God of guidance and shows everything, particularly humanity, the right way, "the straight path."

GOD AND HUMANITY

In order to prove the unity of God, the Qur'an lays frequent stress on the design and order in the universe. There are no gaps or dislocations in nature. The world was created by God's word *kun* ("Be") out of nothing. Order is explained by the fact that every created thing is endowed with a definite and defined nature whereby it falls into a pattern. This nature, though it allows every created thing to function in a whole, sets limits; and this idea of the limitedness of everything is one of the most fixed points in both the cosmology and the theology of the Qur'an. Though every creature is thus limited and "measured out" and hence depends upon God, God alone, who reigns unchallenged in the heavens and the earth, is unlimited, independent, and self-sufficient.

According to the Qur'an, God created two apparently parallel species of creatures, man and *jinn*, the one from clay and the other from fire. About the *jinn*, however, the

Qur'an says little, though it implies that the *jinn* are endowed with reason and responsibility but are more prone to evil than man. The Qur'an, which describes itself as a guide for the human race, accepts the Judeo-Christian story of the Fall of Adam (the first man). The Qur'an states, however, that God forgave Adam his act of disobedience; further, Islam does not accept the Christian sense of original sin. While Christianity states that Adam's violation of God's command in the Garden of Eden condemned the entire human race, Islam holds that Adam's sin was his alone.

The Qur'an declares man to be the noblest of all creation, the created being who bore the trust (of responsibility) that the rest of creation refused to accept. Despite this lofty station, however, the Qur'an describes human nature as frail and faltering. Whereas everything in the universe has a limited nature and every creature recognizes its limitation and insufficiency, man is viewed as having been given freedom and is therefore prone to rebelliousness and pride, with the tendency to arrogate to himself the attributes of self-sufficiency. Pride, thus, is viewed as the cardinal sin of man, because, by not recognizing in himself his essential creaturely limitations, he becomes guilty of ascribing to himself partnership with God (*shirk*: associating a creature with the Creator) and of violating the unity of God. True faith (*iman*), thus, consists of belief in the immaculate Divine Unity and Islam in one's submission to the Divine Will.

In order to communicate the truth of Divine Unity, God has sent messengers or prophets to men, whose weakness of nature makes them ever prone to forget or even willfully to reject Divine Unity under the promptings of Satan. According to the Qur'anic teaching, the being who became Satan (Shaytan, or Iblis) had previously occupied a high station but fell from divine grace by his

Muslims believe Adam and Eve were the first man and woman, just as do Christians. Satan worked to trick them into sin, which has been the fate of humanity ever since. Turkish School/The Bridgeman Art Library/ Getty Images

act of disobedience in refusing to honour Adam when he, along with other angels, was ordered to do so. Since then his work has been to beguile humans into error and sin. Satan is, therefore, the contemporary of man, and Satan's own act of disobedience is construed by the Qur'an as the sin of pride. Satan's machinations will cease only on the Last Day.

Judging from the accounts of the Qur'an, man's record of accepting the prophets' messages has been far from perfect. The whole universe is replete with signs of God. The human soul itself is viewed as a witness of the unity and grace of God. The messengers of God have, throughout history, been calling man back to God. Yet not all men have accepted the truth; many of them have rejected it and become disbelievers (*kafir*, plural *kuffar*: literally "concealing" the blessings of God). When man becomes so obdurate, his heart is sealed by God. Nevertheless, it is always possible for a sinner to repent (*tawbah*) and redeem himself by a genuine conversion to the truth. There is no point of no return, and God is forever merciful and always willing and ready to pardon. Genuine repentance has the effect of removing all sins and restoring a person to the state of sinlessness with which he started his life.

According to Islamic thought, the existence of hell (*Jahannam*) bears witness to God's sovereignty, justice, and mercy and also stands as a warning to individuals and nations of the definitive choice to be made between fidelity and infidelity, righteousness and iniquity, and life and death. The major Islamic schools agree that it is essential to one's identity as a Muslim to believe in and look forward to the day—or, more pointedly, the hour—when God will bring his creation to an end, raise the dead, reunite them with their souls, judge them one by one, and commit each individual, as he deserves, to the joys of the garden (paradise) or the terrors of the fire (hell). According to

Islamic teaching, God exercises complete authority over the course of events. He has predetermined human destiny yet justly holds individuals accountable for their choices in life. Immune to special pleading, God, in his mercy, reserves the power to save those whom he wills and to look favourably upon those for whom the Prophet Muhammad intercedes. Some Islamic schools deny the possibility of human intercession but most accept it, and in any case God himself, in his mercy, may forgive certain sinners. Hell and heaven are both spiritual and corporeal. The damned will also experience fire "in their hearts"; similarly, the blessed, besides corporeal enjoyment, will experience the greatest happiness of divine pleasure.

In Islamic doctrine, on the Last Day, when the world will come to an end, the dead will be resurrected and a judgment will be pronounced on every person in accordance with his deeds. Although the Qur'an in the main speaks of a personal judgment, there are several verses that speak of the resurrection of distinct communities that will be judged according to "their own book." In conformity with this, the Qur'an also speaks in several passages of the "death of communities," each one of which has a definite term of life. The actual evaluation, however, will be for every individual, whatever the terms of reference of his performance. In order to prove that the resurrection will occur, the Qur'an uses a moral and a physical argument. Because not all requital is meted out in this life, a final judgment is necessary to bring it to completion. Physically, God, who is all-powerful, has the ability to destroy and bring back to life all creatures, who are limited and are, therefore, subject to God's limitless power.

The Qur'an has little to say about the interval (*barzakh*) between death and resurrection, but later Islamic literature makes the deathbed and the grave the setting of a preliminary judgment. The soul of the pious Muslim, it is held, will experience an easy death and a pleasant sojourn in the grave. The infidel's soul, violently torn from the body and failing interrogation by the angels Munkar and Nakir, will suffer torment in the grave until the day when it will take up its place in hell, there to dine on bitter fruit and pus and to be roasted and boiled with all the usual infernal devices for as long as God sees fit. Like the joys of heaven, the pains of hell are profoundly physical and spiritual. The worst of all torments is the estrangement from God.

Every destiny is written on the "well-preserved tablet," and now "the pen has dried up"—a change in destiny is not possible. Later mystics have relied on an extra-Qur'anic revelation in which God attests: "I was a hidden treasure" and have seen the reason for creation in God's yearning to be known and loved. For them, creation is the projection of divine names and qualities onto the world of matter.

The central event of Islam is death and resurrection. The dead will be questioned by two terrible angels (hence the recitation of the *shahadah* to the dying). Only the souls of martyrs go straight to heaven where they remain in the crops of green birds around the divine throne (green is always connected with heavenly bliss). The end of the world will be announced by the coming of the *mahdi* (literally, "the directed or guided one")—a messianic figure who will appear in the last days and is not found in the Qur'an but developed out of Shi'ah speculations and sometimes identified with Jesus. The *mahdi* will slay the Dajjal, the one-eyed evil spirit, and combat the dangerous enemies, Yajuj and Majuj, who will come from the north of the earth. The trumpet of Israfil, one of the four archangels, will awaken the dead for the day of resurrection, which is many thousands of years long and the name of which has come to designate a state of complete confusion and turmoil.

According to traditional historiography, Islam is not a messianic religion. Some scholars, however, have suggested that, like Christianity, Islam was intensely apocalyptic at its origins and that Muhammad was the herald of the "day of the Lord." Certainly apocalyptic themes—the Day of Judgment (Yawm al-Din), the Day of Resurrection (Yawm al-Qiyama), the return of Jesus and his fight against al-Dajjal (the Antichrist), and the wars of Gog and Magog—appear throughout the Qur'an. Although they are only now drawing scholarly attention, numerous apocalyptic Hadith (major sources of Islamic law, based on the sayings or traditions of the Prophet Muhammad) have appeared throughout the history of Islam. Furthermore, Shiʻite teaching openly embraces an eschatology that is "this-worldly" (i.e., millennial and messianic), and, although Sunni theology tends to downplay millennialism, it does promote the notion of a line of messianic emperors.

Fairly early on the notion emerged of an eschatological restorer of the faith. Identified as a descendant of the Prophet, he is usually referred to as the *mahdi*. At the Last Judgment, the good will enter paradise and the evil will fall into hell. The period before the End is regarded as a dark time when God himself will abandon the world. The Kaʻbah (the great pilgrimage sanctuary of the Muslim world) will vanish, the copies of the Qur'an will become empty paper, and its words will disappear from memory. Then the End will draw near.

Although all orthodox Muslims believe in the coming of a final restorer of the faith, in Sunni Islam the *mahdi* is part of folklore rather than dogma. In times of crisis and of political or religious ferment, mahdistic expectations have increased and given rise to many self-styled *mahdi*s. The best-known, Muhammad Ahmad (al-Mahdi), the *mahdi* of The Sudan, revolted against the Egyptian administration in 1881 and, after several spectacular victories,

MAHDI

Though the idea of the *mahdi* appeared early in Islamic eschatology, the Qur'an does not mention him, and almost no reliable hadith concerning the *mahdi* can be adduced. Many orthodox Sunni theologians question Mahdist beliefs, but such beliefs form a necessary part of Shi'ite doctrine.

The doctrine of the *mahdi* seems to have gained currency during the confusion and insecurity of the religious and political upheavals of early Islam (7th and 8th centuries). In 686, al-Mukhtar ibn Abu 'Ubayd at-Thaqafi, leader of a revolt of non-Arab Muslims in Iraq, seems to have first used the doctrine by maintaining his allegiance to a son of 'Ali (Muhammad's son-in-law and fourth caliph), Muhammad ibn al-Hanafiyah, even after al-Hanafiyah's death. Abu 'Ubayd taught that, as *mahdi*, al-Hanafiyah remained alive in his tomb in a state of occultation (*ghaybah*) and would reappear to vanquish his enemies. In 750 the 'Abbasid revolution made use of eschatological prophecies current at the time that the *mahdi* would rise in Khorasan in the east, carrying a black banner.

Belief in the *mahdi* has tended to receive new emphasis in every time of crisis. Thus, after the battle of Las Navas de Tolosa (1212), when most of Spain was lost for Islam, Spanish Muslims circulated traditions ascribed to the Prophet foretelling a reconquest of Spain by the *mahdi*. During the Napoleonic invasion of Egypt, a person claiming to be the *mahdi* appeared briefly in Lower Egypt.

Because the *mahdi* is seen as a restorer of the political power and religious purity of Islam, the title has tended to be claimed by social revolutionaries in Islamic society. North Africa in particular has seen a number of self-styled *mahdis*, most important of these being 'Ubayd Allah, founder of the Fatimid dynasty (909); Muhammad ibn Tumart, founder of the Almohad movement in Morocco in the 12th century; and Muhammad Ahmad, the *mahdi* of The Sudan who, in 1881, revolted against the Egyptian administration.

established the mahdist state that was defeated by the British military leader Horatio Herbert Kitchener at Omdurman (in The Sudan) in 1898.

The doctrine of the *mahdi* is an essential part of the creed of Shi'ite Islam (which recognizes the transference of spiritual leadership through the family of 'Ali). The Twelvers (Ithna 'Ashariyah), the main Shi'ite group, identify 12 visible imams, descendants of 'Ali who are the only legitimate rulers of the Muslim community; the last imam disappeared in 847. The Twelvers believe the *mahdi* is the 12th imam, who will reappear from his place of occultation (or *ghaybah*, meaning "concealment by God"). Some mahdist movements began as Shi'ite movements but eventually broke away from Islam to form new religions. The Fatimid caliph of Egypt, al-Hakim, destroyed the Holy Sepulchre in Jerusalem in 1009 CE (AH 400) and claimed to be the final prophet and the divine incarnation. After the caliph's assassination (probably by one of his many enemies), his most devoted followers formed the Druze religion, which teaches that he will return to establish his rule at the Endtime (1,000 years after his disappearance). Other messianic figures from the Islamic tradition include the founder of the Indian Ahmadiyah sect, Mirza Ghulam Ahmad, who in the late 19th century declared himself to be the Christ and the *mahdi*, and the founder of the Baha'i faith, the Iranian Mirza 'Ali Mohammad of Shiraz, who proclaimed himself to be the Bab ("Gate") in 1844 (AH 1260) on the 1,000th anniversary of the disappearance of the 12th imam.

As early as AH 200, belief emerged in another messianic figure, the *mujaddid* (a divinely inspired reformer who was to restore the Islamic community to its original purity). Unlike that of the *mahdi*, the return of the *mujaddid* was thought to be cyclic and was associated with the century's end. Indeed, at the end of every century since AH 200, powerful religious movements with strong apocalyptic tendencies have emerged in the Islamic world. These cyclic apocalyptic episodes are now regarded as revitalization movements and as times of renewal of religious commitment and enthusiasm. But in every case where evidence of belief in the *mujaddid* exists (e.g., with al-Ma'mun in AH 200, al-Hakim in 400, Akbar, the emperor of Mughal India, in 1000, and al-Mahdi in the Sudan in 1300), the millennial, messianic tendencies of the actors are clear.

THE PROPHET'S DEEDS AND WORDS

Muslims believe that Muhammad was the most perfect of God's creatures, and, although not divine, he was, according to a famous Arabic poem, not just a man among men but like a ruby among ordinary stones. In the same way that in Christianity all virtues are associated with Jesus Christ, in Islam they are associated with the Prophet. The ethical teachings of Islam are rooted in the Qur'an, but the model of perfect ethical character, which is called Muhammadan character by Muslims, has always been that of the Prophet. The virtues that characterize him are humility and poverty, magnanimity and nobility, and sincerity and truthfulness. Like Jesus Christ, Muhammad loved spiritual poverty and was also close to the economically poor, living very simply even after he had become "the ruler of a whole world." He was also always severe with himself and emphasized that, if exertion in the path of God (*al-jihad*; commonly translated as "holy war") can sometimes mean fighting to preserve one's life and religion, the greater jihad is to fight against the dispersing tendencies of the concupiscent soul.

These virtues have served as models and sources of inspiration for all Muslims and have been applied on many levels from the most outward to the most inward. The great classical texts of Islamic ethics, such as those of al-Qushayri and al-Ghazali, which are still widely read, are expositions of ethical and spiritual virtues that all Muslims believe the Prophet possessed on the highest level. Along with these works, there is a genre of prophetic biography based on Muhammad's inner reality and ethical character rather than the external episodes of his life.

The deeds of the Prophet, called the Sunnah—which technically also embraces his sayings, or Hadith—are, after the Qur'an, the most important source of everything Islamic from law to art, as well as from economics to metaphysics, and are the model of behaviour that all pious Muslims seek to emulate. At the heart of the Sunnah is what may be called the quintessential Sunnah, which concerns the spiritual life. The Sunnah also covers a broad array of activities and beliefs, ranging from entering a mosque, practicing private hygiene, and dealing with family to the most sublime mystical questions involving the love between humans and God. In addition, it addresses everyday activities, including the greeting that Muhammad taught Muslims to offer each other—*al-salamu 'alaykum* ("may peace be upon you")—a greeting still used in tens of languages from Jakarta to London and from Rio de Janeiro to San Francisco. Intimate matters of personal life as well as the social and economic life of Muslims have been governed over the ages by the Sunnah. Even the details of all the major rites of the religion—that is, the daily prayers, the fasting, the annual pilgrimage, etc.—are based on the prophetic Sunnah. The Qur'an commands believers to perform the canonical prayers, to fast, and to perform the

In the foreground an Afghani man takes off his shoes to enter the mosque for salat al-jum'ah. *He is outside the Jamee Sunni Mosque in Afghanistan.* Behrouz Mehri/AFP/Getty Images

pilgrimage, but it was the Prophet who taught them how to perform these acts along with other religious rituals, such as marriage and burial of the dead.

The Sunnah is also the body of traditional social and legal custom and practice of the Muslim community. In pre-Islamic Arabia, *sunnah* referred to precedents established by tribal ancestors, accepted as normative, and practiced by the entire community. The early Muslims did not immediately concur on what constituted their Sunnah. Some looked to the people of Medina for an example, others followed the behaviour of the Companions of Muhammad, whereas the provincial legal schools, current in Iraq, Syria, and the Hejaz (in Arabia) in the 8th century CE, attempted to equate Sunnah with an ideal system — based partly on what was traditional in their respective areas and partly on precedents that they themselves had developed. These varying sources, which created differing community practices, were finally reconciled late in the 8th century by the legal scholar al-Shafi'i (767–820), who accorded the *sunnah* of the Prophet Muhammad, as preserved in eyewitness records of his words, actions, and approbations, and known as the Hadith, normative and legal status second only to that of the Qur'an. During the Prophet's life and shortly thereafter, his sayings were written down on media such as parchment, papyrus, and shoulder bones of camels. They were also preserved orally by a people whose long poetic tradition had been carried on solely by word of mouth in the period preceding the rise of Islam. In the 8th and 9th centuries, however, scholars began to collect the sayings of the Prophet after devising rigorous criteria for examining the authenticity of the chain of transmission (*isnad*). The result of this herculean task was the Sunni compilation of six collections of sayings known as the *Sihah* (plural of *Sahih*; "correct"), the most famous of which was compiled by al-Bukhari. In the 10th century the Shi'ites brought together their own collection in four volumes known as *The Four Books* (*Al-Kutub al-arba'ah*), of which the most famous was by al-Kulayni, but some Shi'ite authorities believe that Shi'ism also has six canonical collections of Hadith. Most of the sayings in the Sunni and Shi'ite collections are the same, but the chain of transmission differs between them. Sunni Muslims believe that many of the sayings were transmitted by Ibn al-'Abbas and 'A'ishah, but Shi'ites accept only members of the household of the Prophet (*ahl al-bayt*) as legitimate transmitters. There are also a number of prophetic sayings known as *al-ahadith al-qudsiyyah* ("sacred sayings") in which

God speaks in the first person through Muhammad. In general, these sayings are of an esoteric character and have been of great importance in the development of Sufism.

The Hadith (Arabic: "news," or "story") record of the traditions or sayings of the Prophet Muhammad, revered and received as a major source of religious law and moral guidance, might be defined as the biography of Muhammad perpetuated by the long memory of his community for their exemplification and obedience. The term derives from the Arabic root *hdth*, meaning "to happen," and so, "to tell a happening," "to report," "to have, or give, as news," or "to speak of." It means tradition seen as narrative and record. From it comes Sunnah (literally, a "well-trodden path," i.e., taken as precedent and authority or directive), to which the faithful conform in submission to the sanction that Hadith possesses and that legalists, on that ground, can enjoin. Tradition in Islam is thus both content and constraint, Hadith as the biographical ground of law and Sunnah as the system of obligation derived from it. In and through Hadith, Muhammad may be said to have shaped and determined from the grave the behaviour patterns of the household of Islam by the posthumous leadership his personality exercised. There were, broadly, two factors operating to this end. One was the unique status of Muhammad in the genesis of Islam. The other was the rapid geographical expansion of the new faith in the first two centuries of its history into various areas of cultural confrontation. Hadith cannot be rightly assessed unless the measure of these two elements and their interaction is properly taken.

The experience of Muslims in the conquered territories of west and middle Asia and of North Africa was related to their earlier tradition. Islamic tradition was firmly grounded in the sense of Muhammad's personal destiny as the Prophet—the instrument of the Qur'an and the apostle of God. The clue to tradition as an institution in Islam may be seen in the recital of the *shahadah* or "witness" ("There is no god but God, and Muhammad is the prophet of God"), with its twin items as inseparable convictions—God and the messenger. Islamic tradition follows from the primary phenomenon of the Qur'an, received personally by Muhammad and thus inextricably bound up with his person and the agency of his vocation. Acknowledgment of the Qur'an as scripture by the Islamic community was inseparable from acknowledgment of Muhammad as its appointed recipient. In that calling, he had neither fellow nor partner, for God, according to the Qur'an, spoke only to Muhammad. When Muhammad died, therefore, in 632, the gap thus created in the emotions and the mental universe of Muslims was shatteringly wide. It was also permanent. Death had also terminated the revelation embodied in the Qur'an. By the same stroke scriptural mediation had ended, as well as prophetic presence.

The Prophet's death was said to have coincided with the perfection of revelation. But the perfective closure of both the book and the Prophet's life, though in that sense triumphant, was also onerous, particularly in view of the new changing circumstances, both of space and time, in the geographical expansion of Islam. In all the new pressures of historical circumstance, where was direction to be sought? Where, if not from the same source as the scriptural mouthpiece, who by virtue of that consummated status had become the revelatory instrument of the divine word and could therefore be taken as an everlasting index to the divine counsel? The instinct for and the growth of tradition are thus integral elements in the very nature of Islam, Muhammad, and the Qur'an. Ongoing history and the extending dispersion of Muslim believers provided the occasion and spur for the compilation of Hadith.

The first generation had its own immediacy of Islamic experience, both within the life span of the Prophet and in the first quarter century afterward. It had also the familiar patterns of tribal chronicle in song and saga. Pre-Islamic poetry celebrated the glory of each tribe and their warriors. Such poetry was recited in honour of each tribe's ancestors. The vigour and élan of original Islam took up these postures and baptized them into Muslim lore. The proud history of which Muhammad was the crux was, naturally, the ardent theme, first of chronicle, and then of history writing. Both needed and stimulated the cherishing of tradition. The lawyers, in turn, took their clues from the same source. While the Qur'an was being received, there had been reluctance and misgiving about recording the words and acts of the Prophet, lest they be confused with the uniquely constituted contents of the scripture. Knowledge of Muhammad's disapproval of the practice of recording his words is evidence enough that the practice existed. With the Qur'an complete and canonized, those considerations no longer pertained; and time and necessity turned the instinct for Hadith into a process of gathering momentum.

Within the first century of the Prophet's death, tradition had come to be a central factor in the development of law and the shape of society. Association by Hadith with Muhammad's name and example became increasingly the ground of authority. The second century brought the further elaboration of this relationship by increasing formalism in its processes. Traditions had to be sustained by an expert "science" of attestation able to satisfy rigorous formal criteria of their connection with the person of Muhammad through his "companions," by an unbroken sequence of "reportage." This science became so meticulous that it is fair (even if also paradoxical) to suspect that the more complete and formally satisfactory the attestation claimed to be, the more likely it was that the tradition was of late and deliberate origin. The developed requirements of acceptability that the tradition boasted simply did not exist in the early, more haphazard and spontaneous days.

It is clear that many customs and usages native to non-Arab societies prior to their Islamization found their way into Islam in the form of reputed or alleged traditions of Muhammad, though always on the condition of their general compatibility with the Islamic religion. Implicit in this sense in Muhammad's personal example and genius, tradition inferred an elasticity and an embrace large enough to comprehend and anticipate all that Islam in its wide geographical experience was to become.

The study of tradition distinguishes between the substance, or content, known as the "gist" (*matn*) of the matter, and the "leaning" (*isnad*) or chain of corroboration on which it hangs. Muhammad observed, "Seek knowledge, though it be in China" or "Beware of suspicion, for it is the falsest of falsehoods" reveals the *matn* or "the meat of the matter." The formula introducing such a Hadith would speak in the first person: "It was related to me by A, on the authority of B, on the authority of C, on the authority of D, from E (here a companion of Muhammad) that the Prophet said F." This chain of names constituted the *isnad* on which the saying or event depended for its authenticity. The major emphases in editing and arguing from tradition always fell on the *isnad*, rather than on a critical attitude to the *matn* itself. The question was not, "Is this the sort of thing Muhammad might credibly be imagined to have said or done?" but "Is the report that he said or did it well supported in respect of witnesses and transmitters?" The first question would have introduced too great a danger of subjective judgment or independence of mind, though it may be suspected that issues were in fact often decided by such critical appraisal in the form of decisions ostensibly relating only to *isnad*. The second question certainly allowed a theoretically objective and reasonably precise pattern of criteria.

If the adjacent names in the chain of transmission overlapped in life, there was certainty that they could have listened to one another. Their travels were also investigated to see if their paths could have really crossed. Biographies could be built up to show that they were honest men and spoke truly. Comparative study could be made of their reputations for veracity as acknowledged by their contemporaries or indicated by their traditions when compared. The frequency of currency through several sources was yet another element in the testing of traditions. Most important of all was the final link with the "companion," who in the first instance had the tradition from his or her contact with the Prophet.

CHAPTER 3

PIETY AND RITUAL
IN ISLAMIC LIFE

The figure of the Prophet Muhammad permeates the life of the faithful; one cannot understand Islamic piety without comprehending his role in it. All Muslims repeat the Qur'anic dictum that Muhammad was sent as "mercy unto all the worlds" (*rahmatan li' al-'alamin*). People ask for his intercession (*shifa'ah*) on the Day of Judgment, hoping to assemble that day under the green "flag of praise" (*liwa' al-hamd*) carried by him. The benediction upon the Prophet punctuates daily Muslim life. He even appears in dreams (a simple dream of Muhammad has been able to transform the lives not only of saints and mystics but of ordinary pious people).

THE FIVE PILLARS OF ISLAM

Over time, Islamic tradition developed both legends and rituals that bring the believer into a sense of a close relationship with Muhammad. Muhammad's birthday is celebrated throughout the Islamic world during the month of Rabi'al-Awwal—not in the same way that Christians celebrate Christmas but as a major feast. Only in Wahhabi-dominated Saudi Arabia are these celebrations not encouraged publicly but somewhat subdued. In the rest of the Islamic world, the miracles associated with his life, such as the "cleaving of the moon" (*shaqq al-qamar*), the Qur'anic revelation through an unlettered person, his Hijrah, and other events of his life are celebrated in numerous ways. His relics are held sacred, and major edifices such as the Jami' Mosque of Delhi, India, have been constructed around them. His own tomb is, after the Ka'bah in Mecca, the most important site of Islamic pilgrimage, and all other pilgrimage sites—from Moulay Idris in Morocco to the Shi'ite places of pilgrimage in Iran and Iraq to the tomb of Mu'in al-Din Chishti in Ajmer in India—are considered "extensions" of his mausoleum in Medina. Muslims experience the Prophet as a living reality and believe that he has an ongoing relation not only with human beings but also with the entirety of creation.

During the earliest decades after the death of the Prophet, certain basic features of the religio-social organization of Islam were singled out to serve as anchoring points of the community's life and formulated as the five "Pillars of Islam" (*arkan al-Islam*). They are *shahadah*, *salat*, *zakat*, *sawm*, and *hajj*.

The first pillar is the profession of faith, also called the *shahadah*: "There is no God but Allah, and Muhammad is his prophet." One's identity as a Muslim and membership within the Islamic community depend upon this profession, which must be recited at least once in one's lifetime, aloud, and correctly. Further, the *shahadah* must be said with both an understanding of its meaning and an assent from the heart.

The second pillar consists of five daily canonical prayers. These *salat* may be offered individually if one is unable to go to the mosque. The first prayer is performed before sunrise, the second just after noon, the third in the late afternoon, the fourth immediately after sunset, and the fifth before retiring to bed. One must perform ablutions—including the washing of hands, face, and feet—before entering the sanctuary. The muezzin gives the call for prayer, chanting aloud from a raised place in the mosque. When prayer starts, the imam, the learned member of the community who leads the prayer, stands in the front of the *qiblah* (the direction of Mecca), with the congregation standing behind him in rows, following him in various postures. Each prayer consists of two to four genuflection units (*rak'ah*). Each unit consists of a standing posture (during which verses from the Qur'an are recited—in certain prayers aloud, in others silently), as well as a genuflection and two prostrations. At every change in posture, "*Allahu akbar*" ("God is great") is recited. The phrases recited in each posture are fixed by tradition.

In strict doctrine, the five daily prayers cannot be waived even for the sick, who may pray in bed and, if necessary, lying down. In practice, however, much laxity has occurred, particularly among the modernized classes, although Friday prayers are still very well attended. Other prayers, while not ordained as an obligatory duty, are encouraged—for example, nocturnal prayers (*tahajjud*), particularly during the latter half of the night. During the month of Ramadan, lengthy prayers, called *tarawih*, are offered congregationally before retiring.

From its beginning in the 7th century CE, the most important part of Islamic liturgy has been the ritual prayer called the *salat* (daily prayer), in which both Christian and Jewish influences can be seen. This minutely detailed

Muslims prostrating themselves during salat *at the mosque of Mahabat Khan, Peshawar, Pak.* Robert Harding/Robert Harding Picture Library, London

prayer is recited while the suppliant turns toward Mecca five times a day. On Friday, the *salat al-jum'ah* (Friday prayer) replaces the noon prayer. It is celebrated by the community in the principal mosque and includes a sermon (*khutbah*), which partly consists of recitation in Arabic of the Qur'an, selected verses of which form the foundation for an address in the vernacular language of the congregation, and a *salat* of two ritual bowings. Friday sermons often have considerable impact on the opinions of congregants regarding both moral and sociopolitical questions. Twice a year, at the end of Ramadan, a solemn *salat* is celebrated, similar to Friday's.

Islamic prayer is an act of adoration of Allah and thus it would not be suitable to add a request. Before adoring Allah the believer must purify himself by means of ablutions in pure water or, failing this, in sand. The prayer is accompanied by a meticulous ceremonial with prostration of the body (*rak'ah*). The sense of adoration and conversation with Allah has led many spiritual Muslims to the heights of mysticism (Sufism).

The third pillar is the obligatory tax called *zakat*, a word meaning "purification" and indicating that such a payment makes the rest of one's wealth religiously and legally pure. This is the only permanent tax levied by the Qur'an and is payable annually on food grains, cattle, and cash after one year's possession. The amount varies for different categories. Thus, on grains and fruits it is 10 percent if land is watered by rain, 5 percent if land is watered artificially. On cash and precious metals it is 2.5 percent. *Zakat* is collectable by the state and is to be used primarily for the poor, but the Qur'an mentions other permissible purposes: ransoming Muslim war captives, redeeming chronic debts, paying tax collectors' fees, jihad (and by extension, according to Qur'an commentators, education and health), and creating facilities for travelers.

Under the caliphates, the collection and expenditure of *zakat* was a function of the state. In the contemporary Muslim world it has been left up to the individual, except in such countries as Saudi Arabia, where Shari'ah (Islamic law) is strictly maintained. Among the Ithna 'Ashariyah (Twelver Shi'ites), it is collected and disbursed by the scholars (*'ulama'*), who act as representatives for Muhammad al-Mahdi al-Hujjah (the Hidden Imam).

The Qur'an and Hadith also stress *sadaqah*, or voluntary almsgiving, which, like *zakat*, is intended for the needy. Twelver Shi'ites, moreover, require payment of an additional one-fifth tax, the *khums*, to the Hidden Imam and his deputies. It is intended to be spent for the benefit of the imams in addition to orphans, the poor, and travelers.

The fourth pillar of the tradition is *sawm*, the fast during the month of Ramadan, the Islamic lunar calendar's ninth month when, according to tradition, the Qur'an was revealed. Prescribed in the second sura (verses 183–185) of the Qur'an is the fourth pillar of the tradition. The 97th verse of the Qur'an opens with a declaration that it was revealed "on the Night of Power," which Muslims generally observe on the night of 26–27 Ramadan. Fasting begins at daybreak and ends at sunset; during the day eating, drinking, and smoking are forbidden. A person who is sick or on a journey may postpone *sawm* until "another equal number of days." The elderly and the incurably sick are exempted through the daily feeding of one poor person if they have the means.

The fifth pillar is the annual pilgrimage, or *hajj*, to Mecca. It is prescribed for every Muslim once in a lifetime — "provided one can afford it" and has enough provisions to leave for his family in his absence. A person may perform the *hajj* by proxy, appointing a relative or friend going on the pilgrimage to "stand in" for him or her. Many countries have imposed restrictions on the number of outgoing pilgrims because of foreign-exchange difficulties. Because of the improvement of communications, however, the total number of visitors has greatly increased in recent years. By the early 1990s the number of visitors was estimated to be about two million, approximately half of them from non-Arab countries. All Muslim countries send official delegations on the occasion, which is being increasingly used for religio-political congresses. At other times in the year, it is considered meritorious to perform the lesser pilgrimage (*'umrah*), which is not, however, a substitute for the *hajj* pilgrimage.

The pattern of pilgrimage rites was established by the Prophet Muhammad, but variations have arisen in it, and the stringent formal itinerary is not strictly adhered to by the mass of pilgrims, who frequently visit the various Meccan sites out of their proper order. When the pilgrim is about 6 miles (10 km) from Mecca, he enters the state of holiness and purity known as *ihram* and dons the *ihram* garments, consisting of two white seamless sheets that are wrapped around the body. The pilgrim cuts neither his hair nor his nails until the pilgrimage rite is over. He enters Mecca and walks seven times around the sacred shrine called the Ka'bah, in the Great Mosque, kisses or touches the Black Stone (Hajar al-Aswad) in the Ka'bah, prays twice in the direction of the Maqam Ibrahim and the Ka'bah, and runs seven times between the minor prominences of Mount Safa and Mount Marwah. On the 7th of Dhu al-Hijjah the pilgrim is reminded of his duties. At the second stage of the ritual, which takes place between the 8th and the 12th days of the month, the pilgrim visits the holy places outside Mecca—Jabal al-Rahmah, Muzdalifah, Mina—and

The Ka'bah in the Great Mosque, Mecca.

sacrifices an animal in commemoration of Abraham's sacrifice. The pilgrim's head is then usually shaved, and, after throwing seven stones at each of the three pillars at Mina on three successive days (the pillars exemplify various devils), he returns to Mecca to perform the farewell *tawaf*, or circling, of the Ka'bah before leaving the city.

HOLY DAYS

The Muslim calendar, which is based on the lunar year, dates from the emigration (*hijrah*) of the Prophet from Mecca to Medina in 622. The two festive days in the year are the *'ids*, 'Id al-Fitr celebrating the end of the month of Ramadan and 'Id al-Adha (the feast of sacrifice) marking the end of the pilgrimage. Because of the crowds, *'id* prayers are offered either in very large mosques or on specially consecrated grounds. Other sacred times include the "Night of Power" (believed to be the night in which God makes decisions about the destiny of individuals and the world as a whole) and the night of the ascension of the Prophet to heaven. The Shi'ah celebrate the 10th of Muharram (the first month of the Muslim year) to mark the day of the martyrdom of Husayn. The Muslim masses also celebrate the death anniversaries of various saints in a ceremony called *'urs* (literally, "nuptial ceremony"). The saints, far from dying, are believed to reach the zenith of their spiritual life on this occasion.

The Islamic calendar is the dating system used in the Muslim world (except Turkey, which adopted the Gregorian calendar in 1925) and is based on a year of 12 months, each month beginning approximately at the time of the New Moon. (The Iranian calendar, however, is based on a solar year.) The months are alternately 30 and 29 days long except for the 12th, Dhu al-Hijjah, the length of which is varied in a 30-year cycle intended to keep the calendar in step with the true phases of the Moon. In 11 years of this cycle, Dhu al-Hijjah has 30 days, and in the other 19 years it has 29. Thus the year has either 354 or 355 days. No months are intercalated, so that the named months do not remain in the same seasons but retrogress through the entire solar, or seasonal, year (of about 365.25 days) every 32.5 solar years.

One of the basic institutions of Islam, Ramadan is the Islamic holy month of fasting. It is the ninth month on the Islamic calendar. Ramadan begins and ends with the official sighting of the new moon. During the month-long fast, able-bodied adults and older children fast during the daylight hours from dawn to dusk. They also refrain from sexual intercourse during daylight hours.

Fasting, as a pillar of Islam, is essential for Muslims during Ramadan. Ramadan is a period of introspection and prayer that recalls the receiving of the Qur'an, the holy book of Islam. It is believed that on the 27th day of the month of Ramadan, Muhammad received the Qur'an to guide the people. The 27th of Ramadan is celebrated as the Night of Power, or Lailat al-Kadr. On that night, it is said, God determined the plan for the coming year, and Muslims spend extra hours in prayer for the coming year. The holy month is seen less as a period of atonement than as an obedient response to a holy commandment from God. It is a time of communal prayer in the mosque and of reading the Qur'an. Past sins are forgiven those who participate in Ramadan with fasting, prayer, and good, faithful intention.

Muslims fasting during Ramadan break their fast each evening with prayer. They proceed to have festive night-time meals that are often shared with friends and extended family. Some of these festive meals, called *iftar*, last well into the night. The *iftar* usually begins with dates or apricots and water or sweetened milk, and continues through many courses of vegetables, breads, and some meats. The *iftar* is followed by customary visiting of other friends and relatives. In some Muslim communities, bells are rung in the predawn hours to remind Muslims to begin their next day with the meal before dawn, called the *suhoor*. The Qur'an indicates that eating and drinking are permissible only until the "white thread of light becomes distinguishable from the dark thread of night at dawn." The Arabic word for the fast of Ramadan is *sawm*. The word, whose plural is *siyam*, means "refrain." To Muslims, the word means to refrain from all food, drink, and sexual activity from dawn to sunset. The refraining is also interpreted to include all forms of immoral behavior, including impure or unkind thoughts. Therefore, false words, deeds, and intentions are as destructive of a fast as are eating or drinking.

Work hours in some communities are reduced, since Muslims often get very little sleep during the month. *Siyam* can be invalidated by eating or drinking at the wrong time,

During Ramadan, Muslims fast during the day and celebrate once the sun goes down. Here a shopkeeper prepares sweets for the month-long celebration. Sabah Arar/AFP/Getty Images

and the lost day can be made up with an extra day of fasting. For anyone who becomes ill during the month, or for whom travel is required, extra fasting days may be substituted after Ramadan. Volunteering, performing works of righteousness, or feeding the poor are acceptable substitutes for fasting if necessary. Pregnant or nursing women, children, the old and the weak, and the mentally ill are all exempt from the strictures regarding fasting.

At the end of the month, Ramadan officially ends with the sighting of the new moon. The first of two canonical festivals in Islam, 'Id al-Fitr ("Festival of Breaking Fast"), marks the end of Ramadan and the beginning of the month of Shawwal. The holiday begins with the performance of communal prayer (*salat*) at daybreak on its first day. It is a time of official receptions and private visits, when friends greet one another and Muslims visit the graves of relatives. Some cities have elaborate celebrations for the three-day festival of 'Id al-Fitr. Children wear new clothes, and women often dress in white. Special pastries are baked in honour of the holiday, and gifts are exchanged. Families gather for festive meals, and people gather to pray at their mosque.

The other major Islamic festival is 'Id al-Adha ("Festival of Sacrifice"), which marks the culmination of the hajj and is celebrated all over the Islamic world. Like 'Id al-Fitr, it begins with communal prayer at daybreak on its first day. It begins on the 10th of Dhu'l-Hijja, the last month of the Islamic calendar, and continues for an additional three days. During the festival, families that can afford to do so sacrifice a ritually acceptable animal (sheep, goat, camel, or cow) and then divide the flesh equally among themselves, the poor, and friends and neighbours. 'Id al-Adha is also a time for visiting with friends and family and for exchanging gifts. This festival commemorates the ransom with a ram of the prophet Abraham's son Ishmael.

SACRED SPACE

The general religious life of Muslims is centred around the mosque, the public place of prayer. In the days of the Prophet and early caliphs, the mosque was the centre of all community life, and it remains so in many parts of the Islamic world to this day. Small mosques are usually supervised by the imam (one who administers the prayer service) himself, although sometimes also a muezzin is appointed. In larger mosques, where Friday prayers are offered, a *khatib* (one who gives the *khutbah*, or sermon) is appointed for Friday service. Before entering the sanctuary, one must remove his shoes and perform ablutions of the hands, feet, and mouth, lest anything defiling be brought in. Many large mosques also function as religious schools and colleges. In the early 21st century, mosque officials were appointed by the government in most countries. In some countries—e.g., Pakistan—most mosques are private and are run by the local community, although increasingly some of the larger ones have been taken over by the government departments of *awqaf*.

Though the mosque—originally a sacred plot of ground—has been influenced by local architectural styles, the building has remained essentially an open space, usually roofed, with a minaret sometimes attached. Statues and pictures are not permitted as decoration. The *minbar*, a seat at the top of steps placed at the right of the mihrab, is used by the preacher (*khatib*) as a pulpit. Occasionally there is also a *maqsurah*, a box or wooden screen originally used to shield a worshiping ruler from assassins. The minaret, originally any elevated place but now usually a tower, is used by the muezzin to proclaim the call to worship five times each day. During prayer, Muslims orient themselves toward the *qiblah* wall, which is invariably oriented toward the Ka'bah in Mecca. The mosque has traditionally been the centre of social, political, and educational life in Islamic societies.

The holiest site in Islam is the small shrine near the centre of the Great Mosque in Mecca. Called the Ka'bah, this cube-shaped structure is roughly 50 feet (15 metres) high, and it is about 35 by 40 feet (10 by 14 metres) at its base. Constructed of gray stone and marble, it is oriented so that its corners roughly correspond to the points of the compass. The interior contains nothing but the three pillars supporting the roof and a number of suspended silver and gold lamps. The Qur'an says of Abraham and Ishmael that they "raised the foundations" of the Ka'bah. The exact sense is ambiguous, but many Muslims have interpreted the phrase to mean that they rebuilt a shrine first erected by Adam of which only the foundations still existed.

During most of the year the Ka'bah is covered with an enormous cloth of black brocade, the *kiswah*, on which is embroidered in gold the Muslim profession of faith (*shahadah*) and a gold band of ornamental calligraphy carrying Qur'anic verses. Each year during the major pilgrimage (*hajj*), the *kiswah* is replaced with a white cloth that corresponds to the white ceremonial robes of the pilgrims and signifies entrance into a sacred state (*ihram*). At the end of the *hajj*, a new *kiswah* is put in place, and the old one is cut into small relics that are sold to pilgrims.

Located in the eastern corner of the Ka'bah is the Black Stone of Mecca, whose now-broken pieces are surrounded by a ring of stone and held together by a heavy silver band. According to tradition, this stone was given to Adam on his expulsion from paradise in order to obtain forgiveness for his sins. Every Muslim who makes the pilgrimage is required to walk around the Ka'bah seven times, during which he kisses and touches the Black Stone.

Legend has it that the stone was originally white but has become black by absorbing the sins of the countless thousands of pilgrims who have kissed and touched it. When the month of pilgrimages (Dhu'l-Hijja) is over, a ceremonial washing of the Ka'bah takes place; religious officials as well as pilgrims take part.

Muslim theologians have frequently denounced the veneration of relics and the related practice of visiting the tombs of saints (*wali*) as conflicting with the Prophet Muhammad's insistence on his own purely human, non-divine nature and his stern condemnation of idolatry and the worship of anyone other than God himself. Yet a variegated belief in holy men arose because of the demands of popular religion. Because the power and strict judgment of the one, distant, almighty God were emphasized

MECCA

Mecca is the holiest of Muslim cities. Muhammad was born in Mecca, and it is toward this religious centre that Muslims turn five times daily in prayer. All devout Muslims attempt a *hajj* (pilgrimage) to Mecca at least once in their lifetime. Because it is sacred, only Muslims are allowed to enter the city.

Under Saudi rule, Wahhabism was enforced as the state credo, and the facilities for pilgrims were improved. Mecca underwent extensive economic development as Saudi Arabia's petroleum resources were exploited after World War II, and the number of yearly pilgrims exploded. Despite lavish expenditures by the Saudi government to renovate the city and mosque area in terms of both beauty and safety, the overwhelming crush of pilgrims each year has led to tragedy on several occasions, as in 1990, when nearly 1,500 pilgrims were trampled in a pedestrian tunnel, and in 1997, when several hundred more died in a tent city fire and its ensuing panic.

repeatedly, there emerged a desire for intercessors. These were found in saintly men who were believed to be endowed with charismatic powers (*karamat*), allowing them to go miraculously from one place to another far away; to wield authority over animals, plants, and clouds; and to bridge the gap between life and death. The piety of the masses "canonized" holy men while they were still living. After they died, cults of devotion arose at the sites of their graves. Relics associated not only with the saints but also with Muhammad were believed to have special significance. Pilgrimages to shrines were believed to aid the believer in acquiring help and blessing.

For the Muslim masses in general, shrines of Sufi saints are particular objects of reverence and even veneration. In Baghdad the tomb of the greatest saint of all, 'Abd al-Qadir al-Jilani, is visited every year by large numbers of pilgrims from all over the Muslim world.

By the late 20th century, the Sufi shrines, which were managed privately in earlier periods, were almost entirely owned by governments and were managed by departments of *awqaf* (plural of *waqf*, a religious endowment). The official appointed to care for a shrine is usually called a *mutawalli*. In Turkey, where such endowments formerly constituted a very considerable portion of the national wealth, all endowments were confiscated by the secular regime of Atatürk (president 1928–38).

LIFE AND DEATH

Probably no religion deals in such graphic detail as does Islam with the creation, death, "life in the tomb," and ultimate fate of humankind. Yet the Qur'an itself provides no uniform or systematic approach to these problems. Only in its later suras, or chapters, do such problems as the relation of sleep to death, the significance of breathing, and the question of when and how the soul leaves the body get addressed in any detail. Popular Muslim beliefs are based on still later traditions. These are recorded in the *Kitab al-ruh* ("Book of the Soul") written in the 14th century by the Hanbali theologian Muhammad ibn Abi-Bakr ibn Qayyim al-Jawziyah.

The basic premise of all Qur'anic teaching concerning death is Allah's omnipotence: he creates human beings, determines their life span, and causes them to die. The Qur'an states: "Some will die early, while others are made to live to a miserable old age, when all that they once knew they shall know no more" (sura 22, verse 5). Questions concerning the meaning of life and the nature of the soul are dealt with patchily in both the Qur'an and the Hadith. The Qur'an records that, when asked about these matters by local leaders of the Jewish faith, the Prophet answered that "the spirit cometh by command of God" and that "only a little knowledge was communicated to man" (17:85).

The process of dying and the moment of death have been regarded as occasions of the gravest crisis in many religions. The dying must be especially prepared for the awful experience. For all Muslims the standard grave-clothes are the threefold linen shroud, or *kafan*: the *izar*, or lower garment; the *rida'*, or upper garment; and the *lifafah*, or overall shroud. Martyrs, however, are buried in the clothes in which they die, without their bodies or their garments being washed, because the blood and the dirt are viewed as evidences of their state of glory. Muslim custom decrees that the dying be placed facing the holy city of Mecca. Funerary rites do not usually terminate with the disposal of the corpse either by burial or cremation. Post-funerary ceremonies and customs may continue for varying periods. These ceremonies have generally had two not necessarily mutually exclusive motives: to mourn the dead and to purify the mourners. The mourning of the dead, especially by near relatives, has taken many forms. The wearing of old or colourless dress, either black or white, the shaving of the hair or letting it grow long and unkempt, and abstention from amusements have all been common practice. The meaning of such action seems evident: grief felt for the loss of a dear relative or friend naturally expresses itself in forms of self-denial. But the purpose may sometimes have been intended to divert the ill humour of the dead from those who still enjoyed life in this world.

It is orthodox Muslim belief that when someone dies the Angel of Death (*malak al-mawt*) arrives, sits at the head of the deceased, and addresses each soul according to its known status. According to the *Kitab al-ruh*, wicked souls are instructed "to depart to the wrath of God." Fearing what awaits them, they seek refuge throughout the body and have to be extracted "like the dragging of an iron skewer through moist wool, tearing the veins and sinews." Angels place the soul in a hair cloth and "the odour from it is like the stench of a decomposing carcass." A full record is made, and the soul is then returned to the body in the grave. "Good and contented souls" are instructed "to depart to the mercy of God." They leave the body, "flowing as easily as a drop from a waterskin"; are wrapped by angels in a perfumed shroud; and are taken to the "seventh heaven," where the record is kept. These souls, too, are then returned to their bodies.

Islam features a post-funerary custom known as the Chastisement of the Tomb. According to tradition, two angels coloured blue and black, known as Munkar and Nakir, then question the deceased about basic doctrinal tenets. In a sense this trial at the grave (*fitnat al-Qabr*) is a show trial, the verdict having already been decided. Believers hear it proclaimed by a herald, and in anticipation of the comforts of *al-jannah* (the Garden, or "paradise") their graves expand "as far as the eye can reach." Unbelievers fail the test. The herald proclaims that they are to be tormented in the grave; a door opens in their tomb to let in heat and smoke from *jihannam* ("hell"), and the tomb itself contracts "so that their ribs are piled up upon one another." In preparation for this awful examination the roof of the tomb is constructed to enable the deceased to sit up. Immediately after burial, a man known as a *fiqi* (or *faqih*) is employed to instruct the dead in the right answers.

The period between burial and the final judgment is known as *al-barzakh*. At the final judgment (*yaum al-Hisab*), unbelievers and the god-fearing are alike resurrected. Both are endowed with physical bodies, with which to suffer or enjoy whatever lies in store for them. The justified enter Gardens of Delight, which are described in the Qur'an in terms of prevalent, but essentially masculine, tastes (sura 37, verses 42–48). At the reception feast on the Day of Judgment unbelievers fill their bellies with bitter fruit, and "drink down upon it hot water, drinking as drinks the camel crazed with thirst" (56:52–55). They then proceed to hell, where they don "garments of fire" (22:19) and have boiling water poured over their heads. Allah has made provision against the annihilation of the body of the damned, promising that "whenever their skins are cooked to a turn, We shall substitute new skins for them, that they may feel the punishment" (4:56). Pleas for annihilation are disregarded. Although this is sometimes referred to as the "second death," the Qur'an is explicit that in this state the damned "neither live nor die" (87:13).

A Muslim woman reads the Qur'an over her son's tomb. Special care would have been taken to ensure his head faces toward Mecca. A three-day mourning period is required by the Qur'an, though mourning may last longer. Ahmad Al-Rubaye/AFP/Getty Images

Muslims accord a great respect to dead bodies, which have to be disposed of very promptly. The mere suggestion of cremation, however, is viewed with abhorrence. The philosophical basis, if any, of this attitude is not clear. It is not stated, for instance, that an intact body will be required at the time of resurrection. It is unlikely, moreover, that the abhorrence—which Orthodox Jews share—arose out of a desire to differentiate Islamic practices from those of other "People of the Book" (i.e., Jews and Christians). The attitude toward dead bodies has had practical consequences; for instance, in relation to medical education. It is almost impossible to carry out postmortem examinations in many Islamic countries. Medical students in Saudi

Arabia, for example, study anatomy on corpses imported from non-Islamic countries. They learn pathology only from textbooks; many complete their medical training never having seen a real brain destroyed by a real cerebral hemorrhage.

In 1982 organ donation after death was declared *halal* ("permissible") by the Senior Ulama Commission, the highest religious authority on such matters in Saudi Arabia (and hence throughout the Islamic world). Tales inculcated in childhood continue, however, to influence public attitudes in Islamic nations. The widely told story of how the Prophet's uncle Hamzah was murdered by the heathen Hind, who then opened the murdered man's belly and chewed up his liver, has slowed public acceptance of liver transplantation. Kidney transplantation is more acceptable, perhaps because the Hadith explicitly states that those entering the Garden will never more urinate.

CHAPTER 4

COMMUNITY AND SOCIETY

F rom Islam's very beginning, the Prophet Muhammad had inculcated a sense of brotherhood and a bond of faith among his followers, both of which helped to develop among them a feeling of close relationship that was accentuated by their experiences of persecution as a nascent community in Mecca. The strong attachment to the tenets of the Qur'anic revelation and the conspicuous socioeconomic content of Islamic religious practices cemented this bond of faith. In 622, when the Prophet migrated to Medina, his preaching was soon accepted, and the community-state of Islam emerged. During this early period, Islam acquired its characteristic ethos as a religion uniting in itself both the spiritual and temporal aspects of life and seeking to regulate not only the individual's relationship to God through his conscience but human relationships in a social setting as well. Thus, there is not only an Islamic religious institution but also an Islamic law, state, and other institutions governing society. Not until the 20th century were the religious (private) and the secular (public) distinguished by some Muslim thinkers and separated formally in certain places, such as Turkey after the fall of the Ottoman Empire.

ISLAM AND COMMUNITY

The dual religious and social character of Islam, expressing itself in one way as a religious community commissioned by God to bring its own value system to the world through the jihad ("exertion," commonly translated as "holy war" or "holy struggle"), explains the astonishing success of the early generations of Muslims. Within a century after the Prophet's death in 632, they had brought a large part of the globe—from Spain across Central Asia to India—under a new Arab Muslim empire.

The period of Islamic conquests and empire building marks the first phase of the expansion of Islam as a religion. Islam's essential egalitarianism within the community of the faithful and its official discrimination against the followers of other religions won rapid converts. Unlike pagans, who were required to accept Islam or die, Jews and Christians (People of the Book) were assigned a special status as communities possessing scriptures. *Dhimmi*s, protected non-Muslims, were guaranteed the right to life, property, and practice of religion, though they were required to pay a per capita tax called *jizyah*. Further, they were subject to other legal restrictions, including wearing clothing that indicated their status. The same status of the People of the Book was later extended to Zoroastrians, Buddhists, and Hindus, but many People of the Book joined Islam in order to escape the disability of the *jizyah*. A much more massive expansion of Islam after the 12th century was inaugurated by the Sufis (mystics), who were mainly responsible for the religion's spread in India, Central Asia, Turkey, and sub-Saharan Africa.

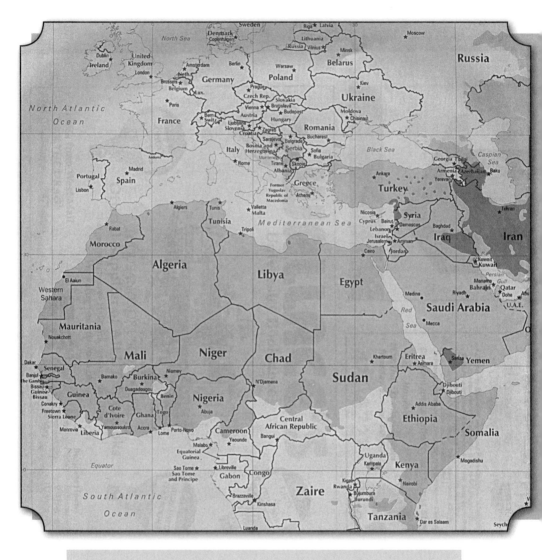

The shaded gray areas on this map (see key) show the greatest distribution of Islam in the Eastern Hemisphere. Note the Sunni and Shi'ite distributions. Courtesy of the University of Texas Libraries, the University of Texas at Austin

Besides the jihad and Sufi missionary activity, another factor in the spread of Islam was the far-ranging influence of Muslim traders, who not only introduced Islam quite early to the Indian east coast and South India but also

proved to be the main catalytic agents (apart from the Sufis) in converting people to Islam in Indonesia, Malaysia, and China. Islam was introduced to Indonesia in the 14th century, hardly having time to consolidate itself there politically before coming under Dutch colonial domination.

The vast variety of cultures embraced by Islam, encompassing more than 1 billion persons worldwide, has produced important internal differences. All segments of Muslim society, however, are bound by a common faith and a sense of belonging to a single community. With the loss of political power during the period of Western colonialism in the 19th and 20th centuries, the concept of the Islamic community (*ummah*), instead of weakening, became stronger. The faith of Islam helped various Muslim peoples in their struggle to gain political freedom in the mid-20th century, and the unity of Islam contributed to later political solidarity.

The doctrine of social service, in terms of alleviating suffering and helping the needy, constitutes an integral part of Islamic teaching. Praying to God and other religious acts are deemed to be incomplete in the absence of active service to the needy. In regard to this matter, the Qur'anic criticisms of human nature become very sharp: "Man is by nature timid; when evil befalls him, he panics, but when good things come to him he prevents them from reaching

Muslim men serve food to the poor. Zakat is a way of life for Muslims, as one of the five Pillars of Islam. Shah Marai/AFP/Getty Images

others." It is Satan who whispers into man's ears that by spending for others he will become poor. God, on the contrary, promises prosperity in exchange for such expenditure, which constitutes a credit with God and grows much more than the money people invest in usury. Hoarding of wealth without recognizing the rights of the poor is threatened with the direst punishment in the hereafter and is declared to be one of the main causes of the decay of societies in this world. The practice of usury is forbidden.

With this socioeconomic doctrine cementing the bond of faith, there emerges the idea of a closely knit community of the faithful who are declared to be "brothers unto each other." Muslims are described as "the middle community bearing witness on mankind," "the best community produced for mankind," whose function it is "to enjoin good and forbid evil" (Qur'an). Cooperation and "good advice" within the community are emphasized, and a person who deliberately tries to harm the interests of the community is to be given exemplary punishment. Opponents from within the community are to be fought and reduced with armed force, if issues cannot be settled by persuasion and arbitration.

Because the mission of the community is to "enjoin good and forbid evil" so that "there is no mischief and corruption" on Earth, the doctrine of jihad is the logical outcome. For the early community it was a basic religious concept. The lesser jihad, or holy striving, means an active struggle using armed force whenever necessary. The object of jihad is not the conversion of individuals to Islam but rather the gaining of political control over the collective affairs of societies to run them in accordance with the principles of Islam. Individual conversions occur as a by-product of this process when the power structure passes into the hands of the Muslim community. In fact, according to strict Muslim doctrine, conversions "by force" are forbidden, because after the revelation of the Qur'an "good and evil have become distinct," so that one may follow whichever one may prefer. It is also strictly prohibited to wage wars for the sake of acquiring worldly glory, power, and rule. With the establishment of the Muslim empire, however, the doctrine of the lesser jihad was modified by the leaders of the community. Their main concern had become the consolidation of the empire and its administration, and thus they interpreted the teaching in a defensive rather than in an expansive sense.

Besides a measure of economic justice and the creation of a strong idea of community, the Prophet Muhammad effected a general reform of Arab society, in particular protecting its weaker segments—the poor, the orphans, women, and slaves. Slavery was not legally abolished, but emancipation of slaves was religiously encouraged as an act of merit. Slaves were given legal rights, including the right of acquiring their freedom in return for payment, in installments, of a sum agreed upon by the slave and his master out of his earnings. A slave woman who bore a child by her master became automatically free after her master's death. The infanticide of girls that was practiced among certain tribes in pre-Islamic Arabia—out of fear of poverty or a sense of shame—was forbidden.

Distinction and privileges based on tribal rank or race were repudiated in the Qur'an and in the celebrated "Farewell Sermon" given by the Prophet shortly before his death. All men are therein declared to be "equal children of Adam," and the only distinction recognized in the sight of God is to be based on piety and good acts. The age-old Arab institution of intertribal revenge (called *tha'r*)—whereby it was not necessarily the killer who was executed but a person equal in rank to the slain person—was abolished. The pre-Islamic ethical ideal of manliness was modified and replaced by a more humane ideal of moral virtue and piety.

COMMUNITY FIGURES

After the Prophet's death in 632, the Muslim community and the land and people under its dominion constituted a political-religious state ruled by a caliph (Arabic: *khalifah*, "successor"). This ruler held temporal and sometimes a degree of spiritual authority. The empire of the caliphate grew rapidly through conquest during its first two centuries to include most of Southwest Asia, North Africa, and Spain. Dynastic struggles later brought about the Caliphate's decline, and it ceased to exist with the Mongol destruction of Baghdad in 1258.

The urgent need for a successor to Muhammad as political leader of the Muslim community was met by a group of Muslim elders in Medina who designated Abu Bakr, the Prophet's father-in-law, as caliph. Several precedents were set in the selection of Abu Bakr, including that of choosing as caliph a member of the Quraysh tribe. The first four caliphs — Abu Bakr, 'Umar I, 'Uthman, and 'Ali — whose reigns constituted what later generations of Muslims would often remember as a golden age of pure Islam, largely established the administrative and judicial organization of the Muslim community and forwarded the policy begun by Muhammad of expanding the Islamic religion into new territories. During the 630s, Syria, Jordan, Palestine, and Iraq were conquered. Egypt was taken from Byzantine control in 645; and frequent raids were launched into North Africa, Armenia, and Persia.

The assassination of 'Uthman and the ineffectual caliphate of 'Ali that followed sparked the first sectarian split in the Muslim community. By 661 'Ali's rival Mu'awiyah I, a fellow member of 'Uthman's Umayyad clan, had wrested away the Caliphate, and his rule established the Umayyad caliphate that lasted until 750. Despite the

CALIPH

As outlined on the previous page, the caliph was the ruler of the Muslim community. When Muhammad died (June 8, 632), Abu Bakr succeeded to his political and administrative functions as *khalifah rasul Allah*, or "successor of the Messenger of God," but it was probably under 'Umar ibn al-Khattab, the second caliph, that the term caliph came into use as a title of the civil and religious head of the Muslim state. In the same sense, the term was employed in the Qur'an in reference both to Adam and to David as the vice-regents of God.

Abu Bakr and his three immediate successors are known as the "perfect" or "rightly guided" caliphs (*al-khulafa' al-rashidun*). After them the title was borne by the 14 Umayyad caliphs of Damascus and subsequently by the 38 'Abbasid caliphs of Baghdad, whose dynasty fell before the Mongols in 1258. There were titular caliphs of 'Abbasid descent in Cairo under the Mamluks from 1258 until 1517, when the last caliph was captured by the Ottoman sultan Selim I. The Ottoman sultans then claimed the title and used it until it was abolished by the Turkish Republic on March 3, 1924.

After the fall of the Umayyad dynasty at Damascus (750), the title of caliph was also assumed by the Spanish branch of the family who ruled in Spain at Córdoba (755–1031), and it was also assumed by the Fatimid rulers of Egypt (909–1171), who claimed to descend from Fatimah (daughter of Muhammad) and her husband, 'Ali.

According to the Shi'ite Muslims, who call the supreme office the "imamate," or leadership, no caliph is legitimate unless he is a lineal descendant of the Prophet Muhammad. The Sunnis insist that the office belongs to the tribe of Quraysh, to which Muhammad himself belonged, but this condition would have vitiated the claim of the Turkish sultans, who held the office after the last 'Abbasid caliph of Cairo transferred it to Selim I.

largely successful reign of Mu'awiyah, tribal and sectarian disputes erupted after his death. There were three caliphs between 680 and 685, and only by nearly 20 years of military campaigning did the next one, 'Abd al-Malik, succeed in reestablishing the authority of the Umayyad capital of Damascus. 'Abd al-Malik is also remembered for building the Dome of the Rock in Jerusalem. Under his son al-Walid (705–715), Muslim forces took permanent possession of North Africa, converted the native Berbers to Islam, and overran most of the Iberian Peninsula as the Visigothic kingdom there collapsed. Progress was also made in the east with settlement in the Indus River valley. Umayyad power had never been firmly seated, however, and the

Palestinians pray outside the Dome of the Rock, at the al-Aqsa Mosque in Jersualem. The Dome of the Rock, the oldest existing Islamic building in the world, is one of Islam's most sacred places. Ahmad Gharabli/AFP/ Getty Images

Caliphate disintegrated rapidly after the long reign of Hisham (724–743). A serious rebellion broke out against the Umayyads in 747, and in 750 the last Umayyad caliph, Marwan II, was defeated in the Battle of Great Zab by the followers of the ʿAbbasid family.

Descendants of an uncle of Muhammad, the ʿAbbasids owed the success of their revolt in large part to their appeal to various pietistic, extremist, or merely disgruntled groups and in particular to the aid of the Shiʿites, a major dissident party that held that the Caliphate belonged by right to the descendants of ʿAli. That the ʿAbbasids disappointed the expectations of the Shiʿites by taking the Caliphate for themselves left the Shiʿites to evolve into a sect, permanently hostile to the orthodox Sunni majority, that would periodically threaten the established government by revolt. The first ʿAbbasid caliph, al-Saffah (749–754), ordered the elimination of the entire Umayyad clan; the only Umayyad of note who escaped was ʿAbd al-Rahman, who made his way to Spain and established an Umayyad dynasty that lasted until 1031.

The period 786–861, and especially the caliphates of Harun (786–809) and al-Maʾmun (813–833), is accounted the height of ʿAbbasid rule. The eastward orientation of the dynasty was demonstrated by al-Mansur's removal of the capital to Baghdad in 762–763 and by the later caliphs' policy of marrying non-Arabs and recruiting Turks, Slavs, and other non-Arabs as palace guards. Under al-Maʾmun, the intellectual and artistic heritage of Iran (Persia) was cultivated, and Persian administrators assumed important posts in the Caliphate's administration. After 861, anarchy and rebellion shook the empire. Tunisia and eastern Iran came under the control of hereditary governors who made token acknowledgment of Baghdad's suzerainty. Other provinces became less reliable sources of revenue. Shiʿite and similar groups, including the Qarmatians in Syria and the Fatimids in North Africa, challenged 'Abbasid rule on religious as well as political grounds.

'Abbasid power ended in 945, when the Buyids, a family of rough tribesmen from northwestern Iran, took Baghdad under their rule. They retained the 'Abbasid caliphs as figureheads. The Samanid dynasty that arose in Khorasan and Transoxania and the Ghaznavids in Central Asia and the Ganges River basin similarly acknowledged the 'Abbasid caliphs as spiritual leaders of Sunni Islam. On the other hand, the Fatimids proclaimed a new caliphate in 920 in their capital of al-Mahdiyah in Tunisia and castigated the 'Abbasids as usurpers; the Umayyad ruler in Spain, 'Abd al-Rahman III, adopted the title of caliph in 928 in opposition to both the 'Abbasids and the Fatimids. Nominal 'Abbasid authority was restored to Egypt by Saladin in 1171. By that time, the 'Abbasids had begun to regain some semblance of their former power, as the Seljuq dynasty of sultans in Baghdad, which had replaced the Buyids in 1055, itself began to decay. The caliph al-Nasir (1180–1225) achieved a certain success in dealing diplomatically with various threats from the East, but al-Musta'sim (1242–58) had no such success and was murdered in the Mongol sack of Baghdad that ended the 'Abbasid line in that city. A scion of the family was invited a few years later to establish a puppet caliphate in Cairo that lasted until 1517, but it exercised no power whatever. The rulers of the Ottoman Empire claimed to continue the Caliphate, but it was replaced with a secular republic founded by Atatürk in 1924.

The head of the Muslim community is called the imam (literally, "leader"). In contemporary Islam, an imam is the person chosen to lead prayer. The imam is appointed by the community based on his learning. The title has a long history of a broader use. It is used in the Qur'an several times to refer to leaders and to Abraham. The origin and basis of the office of imam was conceived differently by various sections of the Muslim community, this difference providing part of the political and religious basis for the split into Sunni and Shi'ite Islam. Among Sunnis, imam was synonymous with caliph, designating the successor of Muhammad, who assumed his administrative and political, but not religious, functions. He was appointed by men and, although liable to error, was to be obeyed even though he personally sinned, provided he maintained the ordinances of Islam.

Political disagreement over succession to his office after the death (661) of 'Ali, the fourth caliph and Muhammad's son-in-law, propelled the Shi'ite imam along a separate course of development, as partisans of 'Ali attempted to preserve leadership of the entire Muslim community among the descendants of 'Ali. In Shi'ite Islam, the imam became a figure of absolute spiritual authority and fundamental importance. 'Ali and the successive imams, who are believed by Shi'ism to be the sole possessors of secret insights into the Qur'an given them by Muhammad, under Neoplatonic influences of the 9th–10th centuries became viewed as men illumined by the Primeval Light, God, and as divinely appointed and preserved from sin. They alone, and not the general consensus of the community (*ijma*) essential to Sunni Islam, determined matters of doctrinal importance and interpreted revelation. With the historical disappearance (*ghaybah*) of the last imam—there has been no consistency in the number legitimized: among the major sects, Sab'iyah Isma'ilis acknowledge 7 imams and Ithna 'Ashari (Twelvers) acknowledge 12—there arose a belief in the hidden imam, who is identified with the *mahdi*.

Sheikh is an Arabic title of respect dating from pre-Islamic antiquity; it strictly means a venerable man more than 50 years old. The title *sheikh* is especially borne by heads of religious orders, heads of colleges, such as Al-Azhar University in Cairo, chiefs of tribes, and headmen of villages and of separate quarters of towns. It is also applied to learned men, especially members of the class of *'ulama'* (scholars), and has been applied to anyone who has memorized the whole Qur'an, however young he might be.

Sheikh al-jabal ("the mountain chief") was a popular term for the head of the Assassins and was mistranslated by the Crusaders as "the old man of the mountain." By far the most important title was *sheikh al-islam*, which by the 11th century was given to eminent *'ulama'* and mystics and by the 15th century was open to any outstanding mufti (canonical lawyer). In the Ottoman Empire the use of this title was restricted by Süleyman I (1520–66) to the mufti of Istanbul, who, equal in rank to the grand vizier, was head of the religious institutions that controlled law, justice, religion, and education. Because of his right to issue binding fatwas (Islamic legal opinions), this official came to wield great power. In 1924, under the Turkish Republic, the last vestiges of the institution were abolished.

The learned of Islam are those who possess the quality of *'ilm*, "learning," in its widest sense. From the *'ulama'*, who are versed theoretically and practically in the Muslim sciences, come the religious teachers of the Islamic community—theologians (mutakallimun), canon lawyers (muftis), judges (qadis), professors—and high state religious officials like the *sheikh al-islam*. In a narrower sense, *'ulama'* may refer to a council of learned men holding government appointments in a Muslim state.

Süleyman I was the tenth and longest-reigning sultan of the Ottoman Empire. He reigned at the height of Ottoman power and was known as Süleyman the Magnificent and as the Lawgiver. Time & Life Pictures/Getty Images

Historically, the *'ulama'* have been a powerful class, and in early Islam it was their consensus (*ijma'*) on theological and juridical problems that determined the communal practices of future generations. Their authority over the community was so pervasive that Muslim governments always attempted to secure their support; in the Ottoman and Mughal empires they sometimes decisively influenced important policies. Although there is no priesthood in Islam, and every believer may perform priestly functions such as leading the liturgical prayer, the *'ulama'* have played a clerical role in Islamic society. Hence they are sometimes referred to as the "Muslim priests."

In modern times the *'ulama'* have gradually lost ground to the new Western-educated classes. Although they have been abolished in Turkey, their hold on the conservative masses in the rest of the Muslim world remains firm. One of the most crucial problems facing 21st-century Islam is the integration of the *'ulama'* and the modern laity.

An Islamic legal authority who gives a formal legal opinion (fatwa) in answer to an inquiry by a private individual or judge is called a mufti. A fatwa usually requires knowledge of the Qur'an and Hadith (narratives concerning the Prophet's life and sayings), as well as knowledge of exegesis and collected precedents, and might be a pronouncement on some problematic legal matter. Under the Ottoman Empire, the mufti of Istanbul, the *sheikh al-islam*, ranked as Islam's foremost legal authority, theoretically presiding over the whole judicial and theological hierarchy. The development of civil codes in most Islamic countries, however, has tended to restrict the authority of mufti to cases involving personal status, such as inheritance, marriage, and divorce; and even in this area, the prerogatives of the mufti are in some cases circumscribed by modern legislation.

OTTOMAN EMPIRE

The Ottoman Empire was created by Turkish tribes in Anatolia. It lasted from the decline of the Byzantine Empire in the 14th century until the establishment of Turkey as a republic in 1922. It was named for Osman (Arabic: 'Uthman), an emir (prince) in Bithynia who began the conquest of neighbouring regions and who founded the empire's dynasty about 1300.

Of the many unique military and administrative forms evolved by the Ottomans, the most notable included the *devsirme* system, whereby Christian youths from the Balkans were drafted and converted to Islam for a lifetime of service. The military arm supplied by the *devsirme* system was the Janissary corps, an infantry group attached to the person of the sultan. Mehmed II developed the practice of requiring all members of the government and army, Turkish or Balkan, Muslim or non-Muslim, to accept the status of personal slave of the sultan. By that means he hoped to ensure the indivisibility of power, with the entire ruling class sworn to absolute obedience.

Under Selim I (1512–20) Ottoman expansion resumed. His defeat of the Mamluks in 1516–17 doubled the size of the empire at a stroke by adding to it Syria, Palestine, Egypt, and Algeria. The reign of his son Süleyman I (1520–66), known in Europe as "the Magnificent," was a golden age of Ottoman power and grandeur. After Süleyman's reign, decline set in, largely because of the increasing lack of ability of the sultans who followed him, the ever-increasing power of the *devsirme* class and the tensions it created within the ruling class, the erosion of Ottoman industry, the decline of Ottoman-controlled trade routes with the development of better navigation, and sudden leaps in population and the subsequent decline of urban centres. Reforms instituted in the 17th century were too weak and narrow to arrest the decline. Meanwhile, the powerful nation-states arising in Europe during this period formed alliances to drive the Ottoman off the continent.

By the accession of Mahmud II in 1808, the Ottoman situation appeared desperate. Local authorities openly opposed the central government, while the empire was at war with both England and Russia. In the next few decades Mahmud II reestablished some order with military modernization and governmental reorganization, but the boundaries of the empire continued to shrink. Mahmud's sons, Abdülmecid I and Abdülaziz, enacted a series of liberal and modernizing reforms called the Tanzimat, which were widely viewed in the West as an effort to encourage friendly relations with European powers. Among the reforms were the first comprehensive education system and the westernization of commercial, maritime, and penal codes. The centralization of power removed all checks on the power of the emperor, but in 1876 Abdülhamid II agreed to the first constitution in any Islamic country. Two years later, by the Treaty of San Stefano and negotiations at the Congress of Berlin, the empire was forced to give up Romania, Serbia, Montenegro, Bulgaria, Cyprus, and other territories. Abdülhamid was able to hold the empire together for the rest of the century by reminding Europeans that the Turks within their own borders were kept peaceful by its preservation, but the final years of his reign were marked by revolts, notably that of the Young Turks in 1908. The Balkan wars of 1912–13 all but completed the empire's expulsion from Europe. After disastrous defeat in World War I and a revolution immediately after, the 36th and final Ottoman emperor, Mehmed VI Vahideddin, was overthrown in 1922 and modern Turkey was formed.

ISLAM AND SOCIETY

The Qur'an not only served as a guide in spiritual life; it also guided Muslims on good practices and right living in daily life. A basic social teaching of Islam is the encouragement of marriage, and the Qur'an regards celibacy definitely as something exceptional—to be resorted to only under economic stringency. Thus, monasticism as a way of life was severely criticized by the Qur'an. With the appearance of Sufism, however, many Sufis preferred celibacy, and some even regarded women as an evil distraction from piety, although marriage remained the normal practice also with Sufis.

Polygamy, which was practiced in pre-Islamic Arabia, was permitted by the Qur'an, which, however, limited the number of simultaneous wives to four, and this permission was made dependent upon the condition that justice be done among co-wives. Medieval law and society, however, regarded this "justice" to be primarily a private matter between a husband and his wives, though the law did provide redress in cases of gross neglect of a wife. Right of divorce was also vested basically in the husband, who could unilaterally repudiate his wife; however, the woman could also sue her husband for divorce before a court on certain grounds.

The virtue of chastity is regarded as of prime importance by Islam. The Qur'an advanced its universal recommendation of marriage as a means to ensure a state of chastity (*ihsan*), which is held to be induced by a single free wife. The Qur'an states that those guilty of adultery are to be severely punished with 100 lashes. Tradition has intensified this injunction and has prescribed this punishment for unmarried persons, but married adulterers are to be stoned to death. A false accusation of adultery is punishable by 80 lashes.

The general ethic of the Qur'an considers the marital bond to rest on "mutual love and mercy," and the spouses are said to be "each other's garments." The detailed laws of inheritance prescribed by the Qur'an also tend to confirm the idea of a central family—husband, wife, and children, along with the husband's parents. Easy access to polygamy (although the normal practice in Islamic society has always been that of monogamy) and easy divorce on the part of the husband led, however, to frequent abuses in the family. In recent times, most Muslim countries have enacted legislation to tighten up marital relationships.

One of the traditions of Islam is modest dress. Women in hijab, with the traditional head coverings, or khimar, *is one way that people honor this aspect of Islam.* Sam Yeh/AFP/Getty Images

Rights of parents in terms of good treatment are stressed in Islam, and the Qur'an extols filial piety, particularly tenderness to the mother, as an important virtue. A murderer of his father is automatically disinherited. The tendency of the Islamic ethic to strengthen the immediate family on the one hand and the community on the other at the expense of the extended family or tribe did not succeed, however. Muslim society, until the encroachments upon it of modernizing influences, has remained basically one composed of tribes or quasi-tribes. Despite urbanization, tribal affiliations offer the greatest resistance to change and development of a modern polity. So strong, indeed, has been the tribal ethos that, in most Muslim societies, daughters are not given their inheritance share prescribed by the sacred law in order to prevent disintegration of the joint family's patrimony.

Underneath the legal and creedal unity, the world of Islam harbours a tremendous diversity of cultures, particularly in the outlying regions. The expansion of Islam can be divided into two broad periods. In the first period of the Arab conquests, the assimilative activity of the conquering religion was far-reaching. Although Persia resurrected its own language and a measure of its national culture after the first three centuries of Islam, its culture and language had come under heavy Arab influence. Only after Safavid rule installed Shi'ism as a distinctive creed in the 16th century did Persia regain a kind of religious autonomy. The language of religion and thought, however, continued to be Arabic.

In the second period, the spread of Islam was not conducted by the state with 'ulama' influence but was largely the work of Sufi missionaries. The Sufis, because of their latitudinarianism, compromised with local customs and beliefs and left a great deal of the pre-Islamic legacy in every region intact. Thus, among the Central Asian Turks, shamanistic practices were absorbed, while in Africa the holy man and his *barakah* (an influence supposedly causing material and spiritual well-being) are survivors from the older cults. In India there are large areas geographically distant from the Muslim religio-political centre of power in which customs are still Hindu and even pre-Hindu and in which people worship an incongruous mixture of saints and deities in common with the Hindus. As Islam expanded into India, most South Asian Muslims were recruited from the Hindu population. Despite the egalitarian tenets of Islam, the Muslim converts persisted in their Hindu social habits. Hindus, in turn, accommodated the Muslim ruling class by giving it a status of its own. The custom of *suttee*, under which a widow burned herself alive along with her dead husband, persisted in India even among some Muslims until late into the Mughal period. The 18th- and 19th-century reform movements exerted themselves to "purify" Islam of these accretions and superstitions.

Indonesia affords a striking example of this phenomenon. Because Islam reached there late and soon thereafter came under European colonialism, the Indonesian society has retained its pre-Islamic worldview beneath an overlay of Islamic practices. It keeps its customary law (called *adat*) at the expense of Shari'ah; many of its tribes are still matriarchal; and culturally the Hindu epics *Ramayana* and *Mahabharata* hold a high position in national life. Since the 19th century, however, orthodox Islam has gained steadily in strength because of fresh contacts with the Middle East.

Apart from regional diversity, the main internal division within Islamic society is brought about by urban and village life. Islam originally grew up in the two cities of Mecca and Medina, and as it expanded, its peculiar ethos appears to have developed in urban areas. Culturally, it came under a heavy Persian influence in Iraq, where the

Arabs learned the ways and style of life of their conquered people, who were culturally superior to them. The custom of veiling women (which originally arose as a sign of aristocracy but later served the purpose of segregating women from men—the *pardah*), for example, was acquired in Iraq.

Another social trait derived from outside cultures was the disdain for agriculture and manual labour in general. Because the people of the town of Medina were mainly agriculturists, this disdain could not have been initially present. In general, Islam came to appropriate a strong feudal ethic from the peoples it conquered. Also, because the Muslims generally represented the administrative and military aristocracy and because the learned class (the *'ulama'*) was an essential arm of the state, the higher culture of Islam became urban based.

This city orientation explains and also underlines the traditional cleavage between the orthodox Islam of the *'ulama'* and the folk Islam espoused by the Sufi orders of the countryside. In the modern period, the advent of education and rapid industrialization threatened to make this cleavage still wider. With the rise of a strong and widespread fundamentalist movement in the second half of the 20th century, this dichotomy has decreased.

LAW

All schools of Islamic law, or Shari'ah, whether Sunni or Shi'ite, agree that the Sunnah and Hadith of the Prophet serve as the most important source of Islamic law after the Qur'an. In Islam even a prophet is not by himself a legislator; instead, God is ultimately the only legislator (*al-Shari'*). Muslims believe, however, that, as God's prophet, Muhammad knew the divine will as it was meant to be codified in Islamic law. His actions and juridical decisions therefore played an indispensable role in the later codification of Shari'ah by various legal schools. Muslims believe that Muhammad brought not only the Word of God in the form of the Qur'an to the world but also a divine law specific to Islam, a law whose roots are contained completely in the Qur'an but whose crystallization was not possible without the words and deeds of the Prophet.

The doctrine of *ijma'*, or consensus, was introduced in the 2nd century AH (8th century CE) in order to standardize legal theory and practice and to overcome individual and regional differences of opinion. Though conceived as a "consensus of scholars," *ijma'* was in actual practice a more fundamental operative factor. From the 3rd century AH *ijma'* has amounted to a principle of stability in thinking; points on which consensus was reached in practice were considered closed and further substantial questioning of them prohibited. Accepted interpretations of the Qur'an and the actual content of the Sunnah (i.e., Hadith and theology) all rest finally on the *ijma'* in the sense of the acceptance of the authority of their community.

Ijtihad, meaning "to endeavour" or "to exert effort," was required to find the legal or doctrinal solution to a new problem. In the early period of Islam, because *ijtihad* took the form of individual opinion (*ra'y*), there was a wealth of conflicting and chaotic opinions. In the 2nd century AH *ijtihad* was replaced by *qiyas* (reasoning by strict analogy), a formal procedure of deduction based on the texts of the Qur'an and the Hadith. The need for *qiyas* developed soon after the death of Muhammad, when the expanding Islamic state came in contact with societies and situations beyond the scope of the Qur'an and the Sunnah. In some cases *ijma'* legitimized a solution or resolved a problem. Very often, however, *qiyas* was used to deduce new beliefs and practices on the basis of analogy with past practices and beliefs. The transformation of *ijma'* into a conservative mechanism and the acceptance of a definitive body of Hadith virtually closed the "gate of *ijtihad*" in Sunni Islam while *ijtihad* continued in Shi'ism. Nevertheless, certain outstanding Muslim thinkers (e.g., al-Ghazali in the 11th–12th century) continued to claim the right of new *ijtihad* for themselves, and reformers in the 18th to 20th centuries, because of modern influences, have caused this principle once more to receive wider acceptance.

BID'AH

Any innovation that has no roots in the traditional practice of the Muslim community is called *bid'ah*. The most fundamentalist legal school in Islam, the Hanabilah (and its modern survivor, the Wahhabi sect of Saudi Arabia) rejected *bid'ah* completely, arguing that the duty of a Muslim was to follow the example set by the Prophet (Sunnah) and not try to improve on it. Most Muslims, however, agreed that it was impossible to adapt to changing conditions without introducing some types of innovations. As a safeguard against any excesses, *bid'ahs* were classified as good (*hasan*) or praiseworthy (*mahmudah*), or bad (*sayyah*) or blameworthy (*madhmumah*). They were further grouped under the five categories of Muslim law as follows: (1) among *bid'ahs* required of the Muslim community (*fard kifayah*) are the study of Arabic grammar and philology as tools for the proper understanding of the Qur'an, evaluation of Hadith (traditions or sayings of the Prophet Muhammad) to determine their validity, the refutation of heretics, and the codification of law, (2) strictly forbidden (*muharramah*) are *bid'ahs* that undermine the principles of orthodoxy and thus constitute unbelief (*kufr*), (3) recommended (*mandub*) is the founding of schools and religious houses, (4) disapproved (*makruh*) are the ornamentation of mosques and the decoration of the Qur'an, and finally (5) the law is indifferent (*mubahah*) to the *bid'ahs* of fine clothing and good food.

In the early Muslim community every adequately qualified jurist had the right to exercise such original and independent thinking, mainly *ra'y* (personal judgment) and *qiyas* (analogical reasoning), and those who did so were termed *mujtahids*. But with the crystallization of legal schools (madhabs) under the 'Abbasids (reigned 750–1258), the Sunnis held at the end of the 3rd century AH that the "gates of *ijtihad*" were closed and that no scholar could ever qualify again as *mujtahid*. All subsequent generations of jurists were considered bound to *taqlid,* the unquestioned acceptance of their great predecessors as authoritative and could, at most, issue legal opinions drawn from established precedents. The Shi'ites, the minority branch, never followed the Sunnis in this respect and still recognize their leading jurists as *mujtahids*, although in practice the Shi'ite law is little more flexible than that of the Sunnis. In Shi'ite Iran, the *mujtahids* act as guardians of the official doctrine, and in committee may veto any law that infringes on Islamic ordinances.

Several prominent Sunni scholars, such as Ibn Taymiah (1236–1328) and Jalal al-Din al-Suyuti (1445–1505), dared to declare themselves *mujtahids*. In the 19th and 20th centuries reformist movements clamored for the reinstatement of *ijtihad* as a means of freeing Islam from harmful innovations (*bid'ahs*) accrued through the centuries and as a reform tool capable of adapting Islam to the requirements of life in a modern world.

The universal and infallible agreement of the Muslim community at any time constitutes the third of the four sources of Islamic jurisprudence, the *usul al-fiqh*. This consensus—based on a Hadith in which Muhammad declares that "my people will never agree in an error"—is called *ijma'*. It has been the most important factor in defining

USUL AL-FIQH

Shari'ah, or Islamic law, is derived from four major sources: the Qur'an, the Sunnah, *ijma'*, and *qiyas* (analogical deductions from these three). Law existed apart from religion under the first four caliphs and the Umayyad dynasty and was generally administered through existing pre-Islamic institutions of foreign (Roman, Byzantine, Jewish, Persian) character. Pious Muslim scholars, who were later grouped into the ancient legal schools of Iraq, Hejaz, and Syria, began to reinterpret the law in an Islamic light. Al-Shafi'i completed this Islamization process by establishing a norm for interpretation, the *usul*, but the functions of the individual principles were fixed in legal theory by later scholars.

the meaning of the other *usul* and thus in formulating the doctrine and practice of the Muslim community.

In Muslim history *ijma'* has always had reference to consensuses reached in the past, near or remote, and never to contemporaneous agreement. It is thus a part of traditional authority and has from an early date represented the Muslim community's acknowledgment of the authority of the beliefs and practices of Muhammad's city of Medina. *Ijma'* also has come to operate as a principle of toleration of different traditions within Islam. It thus allows, for example, the four legal schools (*madhabs*) equal authority and has probably validated many non-Muslim practices taken into Islam by converts.

SYSTEMIZATION AND ADMINISTRATION

The fundamental religious concept of Islamic law was systematized during the 2nd and 3rd centuries of the Muslim era (8th–9th centuries CE). Total and unqualified surrender to the will of Allah is the fundamental tenet of Islam. Therefore, Islamic law is both the expression of Allah's command for Muslim society and, in application, constitutes a system of duties that are incumbent upon a Muslim by virtue of his religious belief. Shari'ah (literally, "the path leading to the watering place") constitutes a divinely ordained path of conduct that guides the Muslim toward a practical expression of his religious conviction in this world and the goal of divine favour in the world to come.

Muslim jurisprudence, the science of ascertaining the precise terms of Shari'ah, is known as *fiqh* (literally, "understanding"). The historical process of the discovery of Allah's law was regarded as completed by the end of the 9th century, when the law had achieved a definitive formulation in a number of legal manuals written by different jurists. Throughout the medieval period this basic doctrine was elaborated and systematized in a large number of commentaries, and the voluminous literature thus produced constitutes the traditional textual authority of Shari'ah.

In classical form Shari'ah differs from Western systems of law in two principal respects. In the first place the scope of Shari'ah is much wider, since it regulates man's relationship not only with his neighbours and with the state, which is the limit of most other legal systems, but also with his God and his own conscience. Ritual practices, such as the daily prayers, almsgiving, fasting, and pilgrimage are an integral part of Shari'ah and usually occupy the first chapters in the legal manuals. Shari'ah is also concerned as much with ethical standards as with legal rules, indicating not only what a person is entitled or bound to do in law, but also what he ought, in conscience, to do or refrain from doing. Accordingly, certain acts are classified as praiseworthy (*mandub*), which means that their performance brings divine favour and their omission divine disfavour, and others as blameworthy (*makruh*), which means that omission brings divine favour and commission divine disfavour. In neither case, however, is there any legal sanction of punishment or reward, nullity or validity. Shari'ah is not merely a system of law but a comprehensive code of behaviour that embraces both private and public activities.

The second major distinction between the Shari'ah and Western legal systems is the result of the Islamic concept of law as the expression of the divine will. With the death of the Prophet Muhammad in 632, communication of the divine will to man ceased so that the terms of the divine revelation were henceforth fixed and immutable. When, therefore, the process of interpretation and expansion of this source material was held to be complete with the crystallization of the doctrine in the medieval legal manuals, Shari'ah became a rigid and static system. Unlike secular legal systems that grow out of society and change with the changing circumstances of society, Shari'ah was imposed upon society from above. According to *fiqh*, it is not society that moulds and fashions the law, but the law that precedes and regulates society. Such a philosophy of law clearly poses fundamental problems of principle for social advancement in contemporary Islam. How can the traditional Shari'ah be adapted to meet the changing circumstances of modern Muslim society? This is the central issue in Islamic law in the 21st century.

For the first Muslim community established under the leadership of the Prophet at Medina in 622, the Qur'anic revelations laid down basic standards of conduct. But the Qur'an is in no sense a comprehensive legal code. No more than 80 verses deal with strictly legal matters; while these verses cover a wide variety of topics and introduce many novel rules, their general effect is simply to modify the existing Arabian customary law in certain important particulars. During his lifetime Muhammad resolved legal problems as they arose by interpreting and expanding the general provisions of the Qur'an, and the same ad hoc activity was carried on after his death by the caliphs (temporal and spiritual rulers) of Medina. But the foundation of the Umayyad dynasty in 661, governing from its centre of Damascus a vast military empire, produced a legal development of much broader dimensions. With the appointment of judges, or *qadis*, to the various provinces and districts, an organized judiciary came into being. The *qadis* were responsible for giving effect to a growing corpus of Umayyad administrative and fiscal law. Since they regarded themselves essentially as the spokesmen of the local law, elements and institutions of Roman-Byzantine and Persian-Sasanian law were absorbed into Islamic legal practice in the conquered territories. Depending upon the discretion of the individual *qadi*, decisions would be based upon the rules of the Qur'an where these were relevant; but the sharp focus in which the Qur'anic laws were held in the Medinian period had become lost with the expanding horizons of activity.

Shari'ah is a candidly pluralistic system, the philosophy of the equal authority of the different schools being expressed in the alleged dictum of the Prophet: "Difference of opinion among my community is a sign of the bounty of Allah." But outside the four schools of Sunni, or orthodox, Islam stand the minority sects of the Shi'ah and the Ibadis whose own versions of Shari'ah differ considerably from those of the Sunnis. Shi'i law in particular grew out of a fundamentally different politico-religious system in which the rulers, or imams, were held to be divinely inspired and therefore the spokesmen of the Lawgiver himself. Geographically, the division between the various schools and sects became fairly well defined as the

HANAFIYAH

The Hanafiyah is one of the four Sunni schools of religious law, incorporating the legal opinions of the ancient Iraqi schools of al-Kufah and Basra. Hanafi legal thought (*madhhabs*) developed from the teachings of the theologian Imam Abu Hanifah (*c.* 700–767) by such disciples as Abu Yusuf (d. 798) and Muhammad al-Shaybani (749/750–805) and became the official system of Islamic legal interpretation of the 'Abbasids, Seljuqs, and Ottomans. Although the Hanafis acknowledge the Qur'an and Hadith as primary sources of law, they are noted for the acceptance of personal opinion (*ra'y*) in the absence of precedent. The school currently predominates in Central Asia, India, Pakistan, Turkey, and the countries of the former Ottoman Empire.

qadis' courts in different areas became wedded to the doctrine of one particular school. Thus Hanafi law came to predominate in the Middle East and the Indian subcontinent; Maliki law in North, West, and Central Africa; Shafi'i law in East Africa, the southern parts of the Arabian Peninsula, Malaysia, and Indonesia; Hanbali law in Saudi Arabia; Shi'i law in Iran and the Shi'ah communities of India and East Africa; and Ibadi law in Zanzibar, 'Uman, and parts of Algeria.

Although Shari'ah doctrine was all-embracing, Islamic legal practice has always recognized jurisdictions other than that of the *qadis*. Because the *qadis'* courts were hidebound by a cumbersome system of procedure and evidence, they did not prove a satisfactory organ for the administration of justice in all respects, particularly as regards criminal, land, and commercial law. Hence, under the broad head of the sovereign's administrative power (*siyasah*), competence in these spheres was granted to other courts, known collectively as *mazalim* courts, and the jurisdiction of the *qadis* was generally confined to private family and civil law. As the expression of a religious ideal, Shari'ah doctrine was always the focal point of legal activity, but it never formed a complete or exclusively authoritative expression of the laws that in practice governed the lives of Muslims.

Traditionally, Shari'ah was administered by the court of a single *qadi*, who was the judge of the facts as well as the law, although on difficult legal issues he might seek the advice of a professional jurist, or mufti. There was no hierarchy of courts and no organized system of appeals. Through his clerk (*katib*) the *qadi* controlled his court procedure, which was normally characterized by a lack of ceremony or sophistication. Legal representation was not unknown, but the parties would usually appear in person and address their pleas orally to the *qadi*, whose first task was to decide which party bore the burden of proof. This was not necessarily the party who brought the suit, but was the party whose contention was contrary to the initial legal presumption attaching to the case. In the case of an alleged criminal offense, for example, the presumption is the innocence of the accused, and in a suit for debt the presumption is that the alleged debtor is free from debt. Hence the burden of proof would rest upon the prosecution in the first case and upon the claiming creditor in the second. This burden of proof might, of course, shift between the parties several times in the course of the same suit, as, for example, where an alleged debtor pleads a counterclaim against the creditor.

The standard of proof required, whether on an initial, intermediate, or final issue, was a rigid one and basically the same in both criminal and civil cases. Failing a confession or admission by the defendant, the plaintiff or prosecutor was required to produce two witnesses to testify orally to their direct knowledge of the truth of his contention. Written evidence and circumstantial evidence, even of the most compelling kind, were normally inadmissible. Moreover, the oral testimony (*shahadah*) had usually to be given by two male, adult Muslims of established integrity or character. In certain cases, however, the testimony of women was acceptable (two women being required in place of one man), and in most claims of property the plaintiff could satisfy the burden of proof by one witness and his own solemn oath as to the truth of his claim. If the plaintiff or prosecutor produced the required degree of proof, judgment would be given in his favour. If he failed to produce any substantial evidence at all, judgment would be given for the defendant. If he produced some evidence, but the evidence did not fulfill the strict requirements of *shahadah*, the defendant would be offered the oath of denial. Properly sworn this oath would secure judgment in his favour; but if he refused it, judgment would be given for the plaintiff, provided, in some cases, that the latter himself would swear an oath.

In sum, the traditional system of procedure was largely self-operating. After his initial decision as to the incidence of the burden of proof, the *qadi* merely presided over the predetermined process of the law: witnesses were or were not produced, the oath was or was not administered and sworn, and the verdict followed automatically.

MODERN REFORMS OF SHARI‘AH

During the 19th century the impact of Western civilization upon Muslim society brought about radical changes in the fields of civil and commercial transactions and criminal law. In these matters Shari‘ah courts were felt to be wholly out of touch with the needs of the time, not only because of their system of procedure and evidence but also because of the substance of Shari'ah doctrine, which they were bound to apply. As a result, the criminal and general civil law of Shari'ah was abandoned in most Muslim countries and replaced by new codes based upon European models with a new system of secular tribunals to apply them. Thus, with the notable exception of the Arabian Peninsula, where Shari'ah is still formally applied in its entirety, the application of Shari'ah in Islam has been broadly confined, from the beginning of the 20th century, to family law, including the law of succession at death and the particular institution of *waqf* endowments.

Nor is Shari'ah, even within this circumscribed sphere, today applied in the traditional manner. Throughout the Middle East generally Shari'ah family law is now expressed in the form of modern codes, and it is only in the absence of a specific relevant provision of the code that recourse is had to the traditionally authoritative legal manuals. In India and Pakistan much of the family law is now embodied in statutory legislation, and since the law is there administered as a case-law system, the authority of judicial decisions has superseded that of the legal manuals.

In most countries, too, the court system has been, or is being, reorganized to include, for instance, the provision of appellate jurisdictions. In Egypt and Tunisia Shari'ah courts, as a separate entity, have been abolished, and Shari'ah is now administered through a unified system of national courts. In India, and, since partition, in Pakistan it has always been the case that Shari'ah has been applied by the same courts that apply the general civil and criminal law.

Finally, in many countries, special codes have been enacted to regulate the procedure and evidence of the courts that today apply Shari'ah. In the Middle East documentary and circumstantial evidence are now generally admissible. Witnesses are put under oath and may be cross-examined, and the traditional rule that evidence is only brought by one side and that the other side, in suitable circumstances, takes the oath of denial has largely broken down. In sum, the court has a much wider discretion in assessing the weight of the evidence than it had under the traditional system of evidence. In India and Pakistan the courts apply the same rules of evidence to cases of Islamic law as they do to civil cases generally. The system is basically English law, codified in the Indian Evidence Act, 1872.

Traditional Islamic family law reflected to a large extent the patriarchal scheme of Arabian tribal society in the early centuries of Islam. Not unnaturally certain institutions and standards of that law were felt to be out of line with the circumstances of Muslim society in the 20th century, particularly in urban areas where tribal ties had disintegrated and movements for the emancipation of women had arisen. At first this situation seemed to create the same apparent impasse between the changing circumstances of modern life and an allegedly immutable law that had caused the adoption of Western codes in civil and criminal matters. Hence, the only solution that seemed possible to Turkey in 1926 was the total abandonment of Shari'ah and the adoption of Swiss family law in its place. No other Muslim country, however, has as yet followed this example. Instead, traditional Shari'ah has been adapted in a variety of ways to meet present social needs.

From the outset the dominating issue in the Middle East has been the question of the juristic basis of reforms— i.e., granted their social desirability, is their justification in terms of Islamic jurisprudential theory, so that the reforms appear as a new, but legitimate, version of Shari'ah?

In the early stages of the reform movement, the doctrine of *taqlid* (unquestioning acceptance) was still formally observed and the juristic basis of reform lay in the doctrine of *siyasah*, or "government," which allows the political authority (who, of course, has no legislative power in the real sense of the term) to make administrative regulations of two principal types.

The first type concerns procedure and evidence and restricts the jurisdiction of Shari'ah courts in the sense that they are instructed not to entertain cases that do not fulfill defined evidential requirements. Thus, an Egyptian law was enacted in 1931 that no disputed claim of marriage was to be entertained where the marriage could not be proved by an official certificate of registration, and no such certificate could be issued if the bride was less than 16 or the bridegroom less than 18 years of age at the time of the contract. Accordingly the marriage of a minor contracted by the guardian was still perfectly valid but would not, if disputed, be the subject of judicial relief from the courts. In theory the doctrine of the traditional authorities was not contradicted, but in practice an attempt had been made to abolish the institution of child marriage. The second type of administrative regulation was a directive to the courts as to which particular rule among existing variants they were to apply. This directive allowed the political authority to choose from the views of the different schools and jurists the opinion that was deemed best suited to present social circumstances. For example, the traditional Hanafi law in force in Egypt did not allow a wife to petition for divorce on the ground of any matrimonial offense committed by the husband, a situation that caused great hardship to abandoned or ill-treated wives. Maliki law, however, recognizes the wife's right to judicial dissolution of her marriage on grounds such as the husband's cruelty, failure to provide maintenance and support, and desertion. Accordingly, an Egyptian law of 1920 codified the Maliki law as the law henceforth to be applied by Shari'ah courts.

By way of comparison, reform in the matters of child marriage and divorce was effected in the Indian subcontinent by statutory enactments that directly superseded the traditional Hanafi law. The Child Marriage Restraint Act, 1929, prohibited the marriage of girls below the age of 14 and boys below the age of 16 under pain of penalties; while the Dissolution of Muslim Marriages Act, 1939, modelled on the English Matrimonial Causes Acts, allowed a Hanafi wife to obtain judicial divorce on the standard grounds of cruelty, desertion, failure to maintain, etc.

In the Middle East, by the 1950s, the potential for legal reform under the principle of *siyasah* had been exhausted. Since that time the basic doctrine of *taqlid* has been challenged to an ever-increasing degree. On many points the law recorded in the medieval manuals, insofar as it represents the interpretations placed by the early jurists upon the Qur'an and the Sunnah, has been held no longer to have a paramount and exclusive authority. Contemporary jurisprudence has claimed the right to renounce those interpretations and to interpret for itself, independently and afresh in the light of modern social circumstances, the original texts of divine revelation: in short to reopen the door of *ijtihad* that had been in theory closed since the 10th century. The developing use of *ijtihad* as a means of legal reform may be seen through a comparison of the terms of the Syrian Law of Personal Status (1953) with those of the Tunisian Law of Personal Status (1957) in relation to the two subjects of polygamy and divorce by repudiation (*talaq*).

As regards polygamy the Syrian reformers argued that the Qur'an itself urges husbands not to take additional wives unless they are financially able to make proper provision for their maintenance and support. Classical jurists had construed this verse as a moral exhortation binding only on the husband's conscience. But the Syrian reformers maintained that it should be regarded as a positive legal condition precedent to the exercise of polygamy and enforced as such by the courts. This novel interpretation was then coupled with a normal administrative regulation that required the due registration of marriages after the permission of the court to marry had been obtained. The Syrian law accordingly enacts: "The *qadi* may withhold permission for a man who is already married to marry a second wife, where it is established that he is not in a position to support them both." Far more extreme, however, is the approach of the Tunisian reformers. They argued that, in addition to a husband's financial ability to support a plurality of wives, the Qur'an also required that co-wives should be treated with complete impartiality. This Qur'anic injunction should also be construed, not simply as a moral exhortation, but as a legal condition precedent to polygamy, in the sense that no second marriage should be permissible unless and until adequate evidence was forthcoming that the wives would in fact be treated impartially. But under modern social and economic conditions such impartial treatment was a practical impossibility. And since the essential condition for polygamy could not be fulfilled the Tunisian law briefly declares: "Polygamy is prohibited."

With regard to *talaq* the Syrian law provided that a wife who had been repudiated without just cause might be awarded compensation by the court from her former husband to the maximum extent of one year's maintenance. The reform was once again represented as giving practical effect to certain Qur'anic verses that had been generally regarded by traditional jurisprudence as moral rather than legally enforceable injunctions—namely, those verses that enjoin husbands to "make a fair provision" for repudiated wives and to "retain wives with kindness or release them with consideration." The effect of the Syrian law, then, is to subject the husband's motive for repudiation to the scrutiny of the court and to penalize him, albeit to a limited extent, for abuse of his power. Once again, however, the Tunisian *ijtihad* concerning repudiation is far more radical. Here the reformers argued that the Qur'an orders the appointment of arbitrators in the event of discord between husband and wife. Clearly a pronouncement of repudiation by a husband indicated a state of discord between the spouses. Equally clearly the official courts were best suited to undertake the function of arbitration that then becomes necessary according to the Qur'an. It is on this broad ground that the Tunisian law abolishes the right of a husband to repudiate his wife extrajudicially and enacts that: "Divorce outside a court of law is without legal effect." Although the court must dissolve the marriage if the husband persists in his repudiation, it has an unlimited power to grant the wife compensation for any damage she has sustained from the divorce—although in practice this power has so far been used most sparingly. In regard to polygamy and *talaq* therefore, Tunisia has achieved by reinterpretation of the Qur'an reforms hardly less radical than those effected in Turkey some 30 years previously by the adoption of the Swiss Civil Code.

These are but a few examples of the many far-reaching changes that have been effected in the Islamic family law. But the whole process of legal reform as it has so far developed still involves great problems of principle and practice. A hard core of traditionalist opinion still adamantly rejects the validity of the process of reinterpretation of the basic texts of divine revelation. The traditionalists argue that the texts are merely being manipulated to yield the meaning that suits the preconceived purposes of the reformers, and that therefore, contrary to fundamental Islamic ideology, it is social desirability and not the will of Allah that is the ultimate determinant of the law.

As regards the practical effect of legal reform, there exists in many Muslim countries a deep social gulf between a Westernized and modernist minority and the conservative mass of the population. Reforms that aim at satisfying the standards of progressive urban society have little significance for the traditionalist communities of rural areas or for the Muslim fundamentalists, whose geographical and social distribution crosses all apparent boundaries. It is also often the case that the *qadi*s, through their background and training, are not wholly sympathetic with the purposes of the modernist legislators—an attitude often reflected in their interpretations of the new codes.

CHAPTER 5

BRANCHES OF ISLAM

Theology, sometimes called *kalam*, as a discipline does not play the same central role in Islam as it does in Christianity. Nevertheless, this discipline, usually translated in Western sources as scholastic theology—popularly held to have been founded by 'Ali— has its roots through 'Ali in some of Muhammad's teachings. At the same time, all schools of *kalam* address the question of revelation and the relation of the words of the Prophet to religious truth on the one hand and rational discourse on those truths on the other. Moreover, if theology is understood to be general religious thought, then Muhammad's teachings are even more central. There has never been a Muslim religious thinker who has not been deeply influenced by the words of the Prophet, whose presence is felt in all forms of religious teachings throughout the Islamic world. Islamic religious thought, therefore, is inconceivable without the Prophet, just as Christian theology is inconceivable without Jesus.

FOUNDATIONS OF SECTARIANISM

The beginnings of theology in the Islamic tradition in the second half of the 7th century are not easily distinguishable from the beginnings of a number of other disciplines—Arabic philology, Qur'anic interpretation, the Hadith, jurisprudence (*fiqh*), and historiography. Together with these other disciplines, Islamic theology is concerned with ascertaining the facts and context of the Islamic revelation and with understanding its meaning and implications as to what Muslims should believe and do after the revelation had ceased and the Islamic community had to chart its own way. During the first half of the 8th century, a number of questions—which centred on God's unity, justice, and other attributes and which were relevant to man's freedom, actions, and fate in the hereafter—formed the core of a more specialized discipline, which was called *kalam* ("speech"). This term was used to designate the more specialized discipline because of the rhetorical and dialectical "speech" used in formulating the principal matters of Islamic belief, debating them, and defending them against Muslim and non-Muslim opponents. Gradually, *kalam* came to include all matters directly or indirectly relevant to the establishment and definition of religious beliefs, and it developed its own necessary or useful systematic rational arguments about human knowledge and the makeup of the world. Despite various efforts by later thinkers to fuse the problems of *kalam* with those of philosophy (and mysticism), theology preserved its relative independence from philosophy and other nonreligious sciences. It remained true to its original traditional and religious point of view, confined itself within the limits of the Islamic revelation, and assumed that these limits as it understood them were identical with the limits of truth.

KALAM

The discipline of speculative theology, or *kalam*, was at its early stage a defense of Islam against Christians, Manichaeans, and believers in other religions. As interest in philosophy grew among Muslim thinkers, *kalam* adopted the dialectic methodology of the Greek skeptics and the stoics and directed these against the Islamic philosophers who attempted to fit Aristotle and Plato into a Muslim context.

Several schools of *kalam* developed. The most significant was the Mu'tazilah, often described as the rationalists of Islam, who appeared in the 8th century. They believed in the autonomy of reason with regard to revelation and in the supremacy of reasoned (*'aqli*) faith against traditional (*naqli*) faith. The Mu'tazilah championed the freedom of the human will, holding that it was against divine justice either to punish a good man or pardon an unrighteous one. The Ash'ariyah, a 10th-century school of *kalam*, was a mediation between the rationalization of the Mu'tazilah and the anthropomorphism of the traditionalists and represented the successful adaptation of Hellenistic philosophical reasoning to Muslim orthodox theology. They too affirmed the freedom of the human will but denied its efficacy. Closely resembling but more liberal than the Ash'ariyah was the al-Maturidiyah (also 10th century).

The pre-Islamic and non-Islamic legacy with which early Islamic theology came into contact included almost all the religious thought that had survived and was being defended or disputed in Egypt, Syria, Iran, and India. It was transmitted by learned representatives of various Christian, Jewish, Manichaean (members of a dualistic religion founded by Mani, an Iranian prophet, in the 3rd century), Zoroastrian (members of a monotheistic, but later dualistic, religion founded by Zoroaster, a 7th-century-BCE

Iranian prophet), Indian (Hindu and Buddhist, primarily), and Sabian (star worshippers of Harran often confused with the Mandaeans) communities and by early converts to Islam conversant with the teachings, sacred writings, and doctrinal history of the religions of these areas. At first, access to this legacy was primarily through conversations and disputations with such men, rather than through full and accurate translations of sacred texts or theological and philosophic writings, although some translations from Pahlavi (a Middle Persian dialect), Syriac, and Greek must also have been available.

The characteristic approach of early Islamic theology to non-Muslim literature was through oral disputations, the starting points of which were the statements presented or defended orally by the opponents. Oral disputation continued to be used in theology for centuries, and most theological writings reproduce or imitate that form. From such oral and written disputations, writers on religions and sects collected much of their information about non-Muslim sects. Much of Hellenistic (post-3rd century-BCE Greek culture), Iranian, and Indian religious thought was thus encountered in an informal and indirect manner.

From the 9th century onward, theologians had access to an increasingly larger body of translated texts, but by then they had taken most of their basic positions. They made a selective use of the translation literature, ignoring most of what was not useful to them until the mystical theologian al-Ghazali (flourished 11th–12th centuries) showed them the way to study it, distinguish between the harmless and harmful doctrines contained in it, and refute the latter. By this time Islamic theology had coined a vast number of technical terms, and theologians (e.g., al-Jahiz) had forged Arabic into a versatile language of science; Arabic philology had matured; and the religious sciences (jurisprudence, the study of the Qur'an, Hadith, criticism, and history) had developed complex techniques of textual study and interpretation. The 9th-century translators availed themselves of these advances to meet the needs of patrons. Apart from demands for medical and mathematical works, the translation of Greek learning was fostered by the early 'Abbasid caliphs (8th–9th centuries) and their viziers as additional weapons (the primary weapon was theology itself) against the threat of Manichaeanism and other subversive ideas that went under the name *zandaqah* ("heresy," or "atheism").

Despite the notion of a unified and consolidated community, as taught by the Prophet, serious differences arose within the Muslim community immediately after his death. According to the Sunnah, or traditionalist faction—who now constitute the majority of Islam—the Prophet had designated no successor. Thus the Muslims at Medina decided to elect a separate chief. Because he would not have been accepted by the Quraysh, the *ummah*, or Muslim community, would have disintegrated. Therefore, two of Muhammad's fathers-in-law, who were highly respected early converts as well as trusted lieutenants, prevailed upon the Medinans to elect a single leader, and the choice fell upon Abu Bakr, father of the Prophet's favoured wife, 'A'ishah. All of this happened before the Prophet's burial, which occurred under the floor of 'A'ishah's hut, alongside the courtyard of the mosque.

According to the Shi'ah, or "Partisans" of 'Ali, the Prophet had designated as his successor his son-in-law 'Ali ibn Abi Talib, husband of Muhammad's daughter Fatimah and father of his only surviving grandsons, Hasan and Husayn. His preference was general knowledge; yet, while 'Ali and the Prophet's closest kinsmen were preparing the body for burial, Abu Bakr, 'Umar, and Abu 'Ubaydah from

Muhammad's Companions in the Quraysh tribe, met with the leaders of the Medinans and agreed to elect the aging Abu Bakr as the successor (*khalifah*, hence "caliph") of the Prophet. 'Ali and his kinsmen were dismayed but agreed for the sake of unity to accept the *fait accompli* because 'Ali was still young. After the murder of 'Uthman, the third caliph, 'Ali was invited by the Muslims at Medina to accept the caliphate. Thus 'Ali became the fourth caliph (656–661), but the disagreement over his right of succession brought about a major schism in Islam, between the Shi'ah, those loyal to 'Ali, and the Sunnah, the "traditionalists." Athough their differences were in the first instance political, arising out of the question of leadership, theological differences developed over time.

SUNNI ISLAM

The Sunnis, members of the larger of the two major branches of Islam, regard their sect as mainstream and traditionalist. They recognize the first four caliphs as Muhammad's rightful successors, whereas the Shi'ites believe that Muslim leadership belonged to Muhammad's son-in-law, 'Ali, and his descendants alone. In contrast to the Shi'ites, the Sunnis have long conceived of the theocratic state built by Muhammad as an earthly, temporal dominion and have thus regarded the leadership of Islam as being determined not by divine order or inspiration but by the prevailing political realities of the Muslim world. This led historically to Sunni acceptance of the leadership of the foremost families of Mecca and to the acceptance of unexceptional and even foreign caliphs, so long as their rule afforded the proper exercise of religion and the maintenance of order. The Sunnis accordingly held that the caliph must be a member of Muhammad's tribe, the

Quraysh, but devised a theory of election that was flexible enough to permit that allegiance be given to the de facto caliph, whatever his origins. The distinctions between the Sunnis and other sects regarding the holding of spiritual and political authority remained firm even after the end of the Caliphate itself in the 13th century.

The Sunnis' orthodoxy is marked by an emphasis on the views and customs of the majority of the community, as distinguished from the views of peripheral groups. The institution of consensus evolved by the Sunnis allowed them to incorporate various customs and usages that arose through ordinary historical development but that nevertheless had no roots in the Qur'an.

The Sunnis recognize the six "authentic" books of the Hadith, which contain the spoken tradition attributed to Muhammad. The Sunnis also accept as orthodox one of the four schools of Muslim law. In the 20th century the Sunnis constituted the majority of Muslims in all nations except Iran, Iraq, and perhaps Yemen. They numbered about 900 million in the late 20th century and constituted nine-tenths of all the adherents of Islam.

The issues raised by several early schisms within the Muslim community and the positions adopted by them enabled the Sunni orthodoxy to define its own doctrinal positions in turn. Much of the content of Sunni theology was, therefore, supplied by its reactions to those schisms. The term *sunnah*, which means a "well-trodden path" and in the religious terminology of Islam normally signifies "the example set by the Prophet," in the present context simply means the traditional and well-defined way. In this context, the term *sunnah* usually is accompanied by the appendage "the consolidated majority" (*al-jamáah*). The term clearly indicates that the traditional way is the way of the consolidated majority of the community as against

A Sunni Muslim holy person reads the Qur'an in his home in Baghdad. It is thought that around 85 to 90 percent of Islamdom follows the tenets of Sunni Islam. Wathiq Khuzaie/Getty Images

peripheral or "wayward" positions of sectarians, who by definition must be erroneous.

With the rise of the orthodoxy, then, the foremost and elemental factor that came to be emphasized was the notion of the majority of the community. The concept of the community so vigorously pronounced by the earliest doctrine of the Qur'an gained both a new emphasis and a fresh context with the rise of Sunnism. Whereas the Qur'an had marked out the Muslim community from other communities, Sunnism now emphasized the views and customs of the majority of the community in contradistinction to peripheral groups. An abundance of tradition (Hadith) came to be attributed to the Prophet to the effect that Muslims must follow the majority's way, that minority groups are all doomed to hell, and that God's protective hand is always on (the majority of) the community, which can never be in error. Under the impact of the new Hadith, the community, which had been charged by the Qur'an with a mission and commanded to accept a challenge, now became transformed into a privileged one that was endowed with infallibility.

At the same time, while condemning schisms and branding dissent as heretical, Sunnism developed the opposite trend of accommodation, catholicity, and synthesis. A putative tradition of the Prophet that says "differences of opinion among my community are a blessing" was given wide currency. This principle of toleration ultimately made it possible for diverse sects and schools of thought—notwithstanding a wide range of difference in belief and practice—to recognize and coexist with each other. No group may be excluded from the community unless it itself formally renounces Islam. As for individuals, tests of heresy may be applied to their beliefs, but, unless a person is found to flagrantly violate or deny the unity of God or

'A'ISHAH

The third and most favoured wife of the Prophet Muhammad, 'A'ishah (614–678) played a role of some political importance after the Prophet's death. All of Muhammad's marriages had political motivations, and in this case the intention seems to have been to cement ties with 'A'ishah's father, Abu Bakr, who was one of Muhammad's most important supporters. 'A'ishah's physical charms, together with the genuine warmth of their relationship, secured her a place in his affections that was not lessened by his subsequent marriages. It is said that in 627 she accompanied the Prophet on an expedition but became separated from the group. When she was later escorted back to Medina by a man who had found her in the desert, Muhammad's enemies claimed that she had been unfaithful. Muhammad, who trusted her, had a revelation asserting her innocence and publicly humiliated her accusers. She had no important influence on his political or religious policies while he lived.

When Muhammad died in 632, 'A'ishah was left a childless widow of 18. She remained politically inactive until the time of 'Uthman, the third caliph, during whose reign she played an important role in fomenting opposition that led to his murder in 656. She also led an army against his successor, 'Ali, but was defeated in the Battle of the Camel. The engagement derived its name from the fierce fighting that centred around the camel upon which 'A'ishah was mounted. Captured, she was allowed to live quietly in Medina.

expressly negate the prophethood of Muhammad, such tests usually have no serious consequences. Catholicity was orthodoxy's answer to the intolerance and secessionism of the Khawarij and the severity of the Mu'tazilah. As a consequence, a formula was adopted in which good works were recognized as enhancing the quality of faith but not as entering into the definition and essential nature of faith. This broad formula saved the integrity of the community at the expense of moral strictness and doctrinal uniformity.

On the question of free will, Sunni orthodoxy attempted a synthesis between man's responsibility and God's omnipotence. The champions of orthodoxy accused the Mu'tazilah of quasi-Magian Dualism (Zoroastrianism) insofar as the Mu'tazilah admitted two independent and original actors in the universe: God and man. To the orthodox it seemed blasphemous to hold that man could act wholly outside the sphere of divine omnipotence, which had been so vividly portrayed by the Qur'an but which the Mu'tazilah had endeavoured to explain away in order to make room for man's free and independent action.

The Sunni formulation, however, as presented by al-Ash'ari and al-Maturidi, Sunni's two main representatives in the 10th century, shows palpable differences despite basic uniformity. Al-Ash'ari taught that human acts were created by God and acquired by man and that human responsibility depended on this acquisition. He denied, however, that man could be described as an actor in a real sense. Al-Maturidi, on the other hand, held that although God is the sole Creator of everything, including human acts, nevertheless, man is an actor in the real sense, for acting and creating were two different types of activity involving different aspects of the same human act.

In conformity with their positions, al-Ash'ari believed that man did not have the power to act before he actually acted and that God created this power in him at the time of action; and al-Maturidi taught that before the action man has a certain general power for action but that this power becomes specific to a particular action only when the action is performed, because, after full and specific power comes into existence, action cannot be delayed.

Al-Ash'ari and his school also held that human reason was incapable of discovering good and evil and that acts became endowed with good or evil qualities through God's declaring them to be such. Because man in his natural state regards his own self-interest as good and that which thwarts his interests as bad, natural human reason is unreliable. Independently of revelation, therefore, murder would not be bad nor the saving of life good. Furthermore, because God's Will makes acts good or bad, one cannot ask for reasons behind the divine law, which must be simply accepted. Al-Maturidi takes an opposite position, not materially different from that of the Mu'tazilah: human reason is capable of finding out good and evil, and revelation aids human reason against the sway of human passions.

Despite these important initial differences between the two main Sunni schools of thought, the doctrines of al-Maturidi became submerged in course of time under the expanding popularity of the Ash'arite school, which gained wide currency particularly after the 11th century because of the influential activity of the Sufi theologian al-Ghazali. Because these later theologians placed increasing emphasis on divine omnipotence at the expense of the freedom and efficacy of the human will, a deterministic outlook on life became characteristic of Sunni Islam— reinvigorated by the Sufi world view, which taught that nothing exists except God, whose being is the only real being. This general deterministic outlook produced, in turn, a severe reformist reaction in the teachings of Ibn Taymiyah, a 14th-century theologian who sought to rehabilitate human freedom and responsibility and whose influence has been strongly felt through the reform movements in the Muslim world since the 18th century.

SHI'ITE ISLAM

As noted above, the Shi'ite Muslims, members of the largest minority sect in Islam, trace their heritage to the Prophet Muhammad through 'Ali, his cousin and son-in-law. The son of Abu Talib, Muhammad's uncle, and his wife Fatimah bint Asad, 'Ali was born, according to most older historical sources, on the 13th day of the lunar month of Rajab, about the year 600, in Mecca. Many sources, especially Shi'ite ones, record that he was the only person born in the sacred sanctuary of the Ka'bah, a shrine said to have been built by Abraham and later dedicated to the traditional gods of the Arabs, which became the central shrine of Islam after the advent of the religion and the removal of all idols from it. When 'Ali was five years old, his father became impoverished, and 'Ali was taken in and raised by Muhammad and his wife Khadijah. At age 10 'Ali became, according to tradition, the second person after Khadijah to accept Islam.

The second period of 'Ali's life, lasting slightly more than a decade, begins in 610, when Muhammad received the first of his revelations, and ends with the migration of the Prophet to Medina in 622. During this period 'Ali was Muhammad's constant companion. Along with Zayd ibn Haritha, who was like a son to the Prophet, Abu Bakr, a respected member of the ruling Quraysh tribe of Mecca, and Khadijah, he helped to form the nucleus of the earliest Meccan Islamic community. From 610 to 622 'Ali spent much of his time providing for the needs of believers in Mecca, especially the poor, by distributing what he had among them and helping them with their daily chores.

Both Sunni and Shi'ite sources confirm the occurrence in 622 of the most important episode of this period. Muhammad, knowing that his enemies were plotting to assassinate him, asked 'Ali to take his place and sleep in his bed; Muhammad then left Mecca secretly with Abu Bakr and reached Medina safely several days later (his arrival marks the beginning of the Islamic calendar). When the plotters entered Muhammad's house with drawn daggers, they were deeply surprised to find 'Ali, whom they did not harm. 'Ali waited for instructions and left sometime later with Muhammad's family. He arrived safely in Quba on the outskirts of Yathrib, which soon became known as Madinat al-Nabi ("City of the Prophet") or simply Medina, on the instructions of the Prophet. According to some sources, he was one of the first of the Meccan followers of Muhammad to arrive in Medina.

Upon the death of the Prophet in 632, 'Ali and Muhammad's family took charge of the arrangements for his funeral. At the same time, discussions began concerning who should succeed Muhammad. Both the *ansar*, the people of Medina who had embraced Islam, and the *muhajirun*, those from Mecca who had migrated to Medina, wanted the successor to come from their group. In order to avoid division, the leaders of the community assembled at *saqifat Bani Sa'idah* ("the room with the thatched roof of the tribe of Bani Sa'idah") to choose a successor. After much debate, Abu Bakr was named caliph , the ruler of the Islamic community. By the time 'Ali finished with matters pertaining to the funeral of the Prophet, he was presented with a *fait accompli*. He did not protest but retired from public life and dedicated himself to studying and teaching the Qur'an. He was often consulted, however, by Abu Bakr and his successor, 'Umar, in matters of state. 'Ali accepted the selection of 'Umar as caliph and even gave one of his daughters, Umm Kulthum, to him in marriage.

After the death of 'Umar in 644, 'Ali was considered for the caliphate along with five other eminent members

AL-HUSAYN IBN 'ALI

Grandson of the Prophet Muhammad and son of 'Ali (the fourth Islamic caliph), al-Husayn ibn 'Ali (626–680), also known as Husayn, is a hero revered by Shi'ite Muslims as the third imam (after 'Ali and Husayn's older brother, Hasan).

The details of Husayn's life are obscured by the legends that grew up surrounding his martyrdom, but his final acts appear to have been inspired by a definite ideology—to found a regime that would reinstate a "true" Islamic polity as opposed to what he considered the unjust rule of the Umayyads.

After the assassination of their father, 'Ali, Hasan and Husayn acquiesced to the rule of the first Umayyad caliph, Mu'awiya, from whom they received pensions. Husayn, however, refused to recognize the legitimacy of Mu'awiya's son and successor, Yazid (April 680). Husayn was then invited by the townsmen of Kufah, a city with a Shi'ite majority, to come there and raise the standard of revolt against the Umayyads. After receiving some favourable indications, Husayn set out for Kufah with a small band of relatives and followers. According to traditional accounts, he met the poet al-Farazdaq on the way and was told that the hearts of the Iraqis were for him, but their swords were for the Umayyads. The governor of Iraq, on behalf of the caliph, sent 4,000 men to arrest Husayn and his small band. They trapped Husayn near the banks of the Euphrates River (October 680). When Husayn refused to surrender, he and his escort were slain, and Husayn's head was sent to Yazid in Damascus (now in Syria).

In remembrance of the martyrdom of Husayn, Shi'ite Muslims observe the first 10 days of Muharram (the date of the battle according to the Islamic calendar) as days of lamentation. Revenge for Husayn's death was turned into a rallying cry that helped undermine the Umayyad caliphate and gave impetus to the rise of a powerful Shi'ite movement.

of the community. One of them, 'Abd al-Rahman ibn 'Awf, withdrew but asked that he be trusted with choosing the next caliph, a request that was granted. He questioned both 'Uthman and 'Ali and decided in favour of the former. 'Ali recognized the caliph's authority, according to Shi'ite sources, but remained neutral between 'Uthman's supporters and his opponents. 'Ali even sent his own sons to protect 'Uthman's house when he was in danger of being attacked. When 'Uthman was murdered in 656 by those who considered him weak and accused him of nepotism, 'Ali admonished his children for not having defended 'Uthman's house properly. 'Ali himself was then chosen as the fourth and last of the rightly guided caliphs.

The period of the caliphate of 'Ali, from 656 until his death in 660, was the most tumultuous in his life. Many members of the Quraysh turned against him because he defended the rights of the Hashimites, a clan of the Quraysh to which Muhammad had belonged. He was also accused of failing to pursue the murderers of his predecessor and of purging 'Uthman's supporters from office. Foremost among his opponents was Mu'awiyah, the governor of Syria and a relative of 'Uthman, who claimed the right to avenge 'Uthman's death. In his confrontation with Mu'awiyah, 'Ali was supported by the *ansar* and the people of Iraq. Before he could act, however, he had to deal with the rebellion of two senior companions, Talhah and Zubayr. Joined by 'A'ishah, daughter of Abu Bakr and third wife of Muhammad, the two had marched upon Basra and captured it. 'Ali assembled an army in Kufah, which became his capital, and met the rebels in 656 at the Battle of the Camel. Although a peaceful settlement had nearly been reached before the fighting started, extremists on both sides forced the battle, in which 'Ali's forces were victorious. Talhah and Zubayr were killed, and 'A'ishah was conducted safely back to Medina.

'Ali then turned his attention north to Mu'awiyah, engaging him in 657 at the Battle of Siffin, the most important contest of early Islamic history after the death of the Prophet. With his army on the verge of defeat, Mu'awiyah, on the advice of one of his supporters, 'Amr ibn al-'As, ordered his soldiers to put pages of the Qur'an on their lances and asked 'Ali to allow the dispute to be resolved by reference to Qur'anic rules. 'Ali's army, seeing the sacred text, put down its arms, and 'Ali was forced to arbitrate. He chose an upright observer, Abu Musa al-Ash'ari, and Mu'awiyah chose 'Amr ibn al-'As. After 'Ali lost the arbitration, Mu'awiyah refused to submit to his authority and then defeated 'Ali's forces in Egypt, where 'Amr ibn al-'As became governor.

Although he continued to have staunch supporters, 'Ali's authority was weakened in many areas during the last two years of his caliphate. A number of prominent Muslims even met in Adruh in 659 with the thought of deposing both 'Ali and Mu'awiyah and appointing as caliph 'Abd Allah, son of 'Umar, but they did not reach a final decision. Meanwhile, some of the Kharijites decided to assassinate 'Ali, Mu'awiyah, and 'Amr ibn al-'As. Although the latter two escaped, 'Ali did not: on the 19th of Ramadan in the year 660, he was struck in the back of the head with a poisoned sword while praying in the mosque of Kufa. He died two days later and was buried in Al-Najaf. Along with Qom in Iran, Al-Najaf became—and remains to this day—one of the most important seats of Shi'ite learning and also a major pilgrimage site.

The significance of 'Ali in all aspects of the religious and intellectual life of Shi'ite Islam can hardly be overemphasized. In the daily call to prayer in Shi'ite countries, and in some Shi'ite mosques in Sunni countries where such an act does not cause major opposition, his name is mentioned after that of the Prophet in the formula *'Aliun wali Allah* ("'Ali is the saint of God"). In the annual Shi'ite religious calendar, the 19th through the 21st of Ramadan is a time of intense prayer and supplication, marking the last three days of 'Ali's life. Many Shi'ites spend the nights of this period, called *ahya'*, in mosques reciting both special prayers, many of them attributed to 'Ali, and canonical prayers, the latter usually at least 100 times. The devotion to 'Ali, not only as the heir of the Prophet but also as the first imam and the ancestor of all subsequent imams, has a central place in the religious consciousness of Shi'ism. There is also a vast body of Shi'ite devotional literature in both poetry and prose in Arabic, Persian, Turkish, Urdu, Gujarati, and many other languages related to 'Ali.

A group of Shi'ites called Zaydis differed only marginally from mainstream Sunnis in their views on political leadership, but it is possible in this sect to see a refinement of Shi'ite doctrine. Early Sunnis traditionally held that the political leader must come from the tribe of the Prophet—namely, the Quraysh. The Zaydis narrowed the political claims of the 'Alids (i.e., lineage of 'Ali), claiming that not just any descendant of 'Ali would be eligible to lead the Muslim community (*ummah*) but only those males directly descended from Muhammad through the union of 'Ali and Fatimah (the sect of Muhammad ibn al-Hanafiyyah died out in the 9th century).

Other Shi'ites, who came to be known as *imamiyyah* (followers of the imams, or religious leaders), narrowed the pool of potential leaders even further and asserted a more exalted religious role for the 'Alid claimants. They insisted that, at any given time, whether in power or not, a single male descendant of 'Ali and Fatimah was the divinely appointed imam and the sole authority, in his time, on all matters of faith and law. The more

speculative among them, the *ghulat* ("extremists"), sometimes bestowed practically divine honours on the imams.
The more moderate came, in time, to claim that at least
a supernatural "Muhammadan light" embodied in the
imams gave them superhuman knowledge and power
and that their sufferings were a means of divine grace
to their devotees. To those Shi'ites, love of the imams
and of their persecuted cause became as important as
belief in God's oneness and the mission of Muhammad.
Under Sunni rule, the *imamiyyah* often were violently
persecuted and sometimes protected themselves by
dissimulating their faith (*taqiyyah*), but Shi'ite doctrine
eventually came to hold that the imam, as *mahdi*
(divine saviour), would deliver the faithful and punish
their enemies.

Several other Shi'ite dynasties played important roles
in Islamic history. The emirs of the Shi'ite Hamdanid
dynasty (905–1004) were notable patrons of the arts. One
of their renowned leaders, Sayf al-Dawlah (916–967), who
fought a long series of campaigns against the Byzantine
Empire, was a patron of the great Arab poet al-Mutanabbi,
among others. Overlapping the Hamdanids chronologically, the Buyid dynasty (945–1055) dominated much of Iraq
and western Iran, occupied Baghdad, and for many years
effectively controlled the 'Abbasid caliphate. Such was the
scope of Shi'ite political power during the 10th century
that often it has been referred to as the Shi'ite Century.

Despite the prominence of great Shi'ite polities, however, Shi'ism remained almost everywhere a minority faith
until the start of the 16th century, when Isma'il I founded
the Safavid dynasty (1502–1736) in what is now Iran and
made Shi'ism the official creed of his realm. 'Abbas I
(1571–1629) later moved the Safavid capital to Esfahan and
established a series of *madrasah*s (religious schools), effectively shifting the intellectual centre of Shi'ism from Iraq

to Iran and adding rigour to Shi'ite doctrine in that country. Extreme (*ghuluww*) religious viewpoints and activities were mollified, and the more excessive groups—including those who were important in supporting early Safavid dynastic claims—were sidelined. Over the next several centuries the empire spread, and conversion to Shi'ism steadily continued. By the early 18th century the Twelver Shi'ites had built a large and vibrant following among the Turks of Azerbaijan, the Persians of Iran, and the Arabs of southern Iraq.

By the time of the Safavids, Shi'ite theological and legal doctrine had expanded and matured, precipitating doctrinal disputes that often became vitriolic between factions within the Ithna 'Ashari religious community. One faction, known as the Akhbariyyah, felt that the only sound source of legal interpretation was the direct teachings of the 12 infallible imams, in the form of their written and oral testaments (*akhbar*). Their opponents, known as the Usuliyyah, held that a number of fundamental sources (*usul*) should be consulted but that the final source for legal conclusions rested in the reasoned judgment of a qualified scholar, a *mujtahid* (i.e., one who is empowered to interpret legal issues not explicitly addressed in the Qur'an). The eventual victory of the Usuliyyah in this debate during the turbulent years at the end of the Safavid empire (early 18th century) was to have resounding effects on both the shape of Shi'ism and the course of Islamic history. The study of legal theory (*fiqh*; the purview of the *mujtahid*s) became the primary field of scholarship in the Shi'ite world, and the concomitant rise of the *mujtahid*s as a distinctive body signaled the development of a politically conscious and influential religious class not previously seen in the Muslim world.

Among the Ithna 'Ashari *'ulama'* (religious scholars), a consensus began to form that, in the absence of the Hidden

Ayotollah Khomeini returns to Iran in Januaray 1979, after 15 years in exile. Within a few months, Khomeini had taken over leadership of Iran. Gabriel Duval/AFP/Getty Images

Imam, the *'ulama'* themselves should act as his general representatives, performing such duties as administering income tax (*khums*, "one-fifth") and the tax to benefit the poor (*zakat*), leading prayer, and running Shari'ah courts. Such doctrines were refined over the centuries, and in the late 20th century a Shi'ite scholar in Iran, who was a recognized ayatollah (an Islamic scholar whose knowledge surpasses that of most and whose legal decisions are accepted as binding), Ruhollah Khomeini, expanded that concept, arguing that the *'ulama'* as a group were in fact

RUHOLLAH KHOMEINI

The Ayatollah Khomeini (1900?–1989) was a Shi'ite cleric and leader of Iran (1979–89). He received a traditional religious education and settled in Qom c. 1922, where he became a Shi'ite scholar of some repute and an outspoken opponent first of Iran's ruler, Reza Shah Pahlavi (r. 1926–41), and then of Reza Shah Pahlavi's son, Mohammad Reza Shah Pahlavi (r. 1941–79). Popularly recognized as a grand ayatollah in the early 1960s, Khomeini was imprisoned and then exiled (1964) for his criticism of the government. He settled first in Iraq—where he taught at the shrine city of Al-Najaf for some years—and then, in 1978, near Paris, where he continued to speak out against the shah. During that time he also refined his theory of *vilayat-e faqih* ("government of the jurist"), in which the Shi'ite clergy—traditionally politically quiescent in Iran—would govern the state. Iranian unrest increased until the shah fled in 1979; Khomeini returned shortly thereafter and was eventually named Iran's political and religious leader (*rahbar*). He ruled over a system in which the clergy dominated the government, and his foreign policies were both anti-Western and anticommunist. During the first year of his leadership, Iranian militants seized the U.S. embassy in Tehran—greatly exacerbating tensions with the U.S.—and the devastating Iran-Iraq War (1980–90) began.

the direct representatives of the Hidden Imam, pending his return. Although many Shi'ite divines continued to eschew the mixing of religion and politics, Khomeini's theory of *vilayat-e faqih* (Persian: "governance of the jurist") provided the framework for the establishment of a mixed democratic and theocratic regime in Iran in 1979.

Over time, Shi'ites became a distinct collection of sects, alike in their recognition of 'Ali and his descendants as the legitimate leaders of the Muslim community. Although the Shi'ites' conviction that the 'Alids should be the leaders of the Islamic world was never fulfilled, 'Ali himself was rehabilitated as a major hero of Sunni Islam, and his descendants by Fatimah—who is venerated among Sunnis and Shi'ites alike—received the courtesy titles of sayyids and sharifs.

Shi'ites have come to account for roughly one-tenth of the Muslim population worldwide. The largest Shi'ite sect in the early 21st century was the Ithna 'Ashariyyah, which formed a majority in Iran, Iraq, Azerbaijan, and Bahrain. The sect also constituted a significant minority in eastern Saudi Arabia and the other Arab states of the Persian Gulf region, as well as in parts of Syria, South Asia, and eastern Africa. The Ithna 'Ashariyyah was the largest Shi'ite group in Lebanon, and Shi'ites in that country, as well as in Iran and Iraq, were among the most vocal representatives of militant Islamism. Smaller Shi'ite sects included the Isma'iliyyah, who formed the bulk of the Shi'ite community in parts of Pakistan, India, and eastern Africa, and the Zaydiyyah, who lived almost exclusively in northwestern Yemen. Various subsects of Shi'ism were also found in other parts of the Muslim world.

Gradually, however, Shi'ism developed a theological content for its political stand. Probably under Gnostic (esoteric, dualistic, and speculative) and old Iranian (dualistic) influences, the figure of the political ruler, the imam (exemplary "leader"), was transformed into a metaphysical being, a manifestation of God and the primordial light that sustains the universe and bestows true knowledge on man. Through the imam alone the hidden and true meaning of the Qur'anic revelation can be known, because the imam alone is infallible. The Shi'ah thus developed a doctrine of esoteric knowledge that was adopted also, in a modified form, by the Sufis, or Islamic mystics. The orthodox Shi'ah recognize 12 such imams, the last (Muhammad) having disappeared in the 9th century. Since that time, the *mujtahids* (i.e., the Shi'i divines) have been able to interpret law and doctrine under the putative guidance of the imam, who will return toward the end of time to fill the world with truth and justice.

On the basis of their doctrine of imamology, the Shi'ah emphasize their idealism and transcendentalism in conscious contrast with Sunni pragmatism. Thus, whereas the Sunnis believe in the *ijma'* ("consensus") of the community as the source of decision making and workable knowledge, the Shi'ah believe that knowledge derived from fallible sources is useless and that sure and true knowledge can come only through a contact with the infallible imam. Again, in marked contrast to Sunnism, Shi'ism adopted the Mu'tazili doctrine of the freedom of the human will and the capacity of human reason to know good and evil, although its position on the question of the relationship of faith to works is the same as that of the Sunnis.

Parallel to the doctrine of an esoteric knowledge, Shi'ism, because of its early defeats and persecutions, also adopted the principle of *taqiyyah*, or dissimulation of faith in a hostile environment. Introduced first as a practical principle, *taqiyyah*, which is also attributed to 'Ali and other imams, became an important part of the Shi'ah religious teaching and practice. In the sphere of law, Shi'ism differs from Sunni law mainly in allowing a temporary

TAQIYYAH

Taqiyyah is the practice of concealing one's belief and fore-going ordinary religious duties when under threat of death or injury. Derived from the Arabic word *waqa* ("to shield oneself"), *taqiyyah* defies easy translation. English renderings such as "pre-cautionary dissimulation" or "prudent fear" partly convey the term's meaning of self-protection in the face of danger to oneself or, by extension and depending upon the circumstances, to one's fellow Muslims. Thus, *taqiyyah* may be used for either the protection of an individual or the protection of a community. Moreover, it is not used or even interpreted in the same way by every sect of Islam. *Taqiyyah* has been employed by the Shi'ites, the largest minority sect of Islam, because of their historical persecution and political defeats not only by non-Muslims but also at the hands of the majority Sunni sect.

Scriptural authority for *taqiyyah* is derived from two statements in the Qur'an, the holy book of Islam. The 28th verse of the third sura says that, out of fear of Allah (God), believers should not show preference in friendship to unbelievers "unless to safeguard yourselves against them." The ninth sura was revealed (according to tradition) to ease the conscience of 'Ammar ibn Yasir, a devout follower of the Prophet Muhammad who renounced his faith under torture and threat of death. Verse 106 of this sura proclaims that if a Muslim who is forced to deny his religion is nevertheless a true believer who feels "the peace of faith" in his heart, he will not suffer great punishment (16:106). The meaning of these verses is not clear even in the context of the sura in which they appear. Thus, even among Islamic scholars who agree that the verses provide Qur'anic sanction for *taqiyyah*, there is considerable disagreement about how the verses do this and about what *taqiyyah* permits in practice.

The Hadith has also been cited as providing theological warrant for *taqiyyah*. One hadith in particular mentions that Muhammad waited 13 years, until he could "gain a sufficient number of loyal supporters," before combating his powerful polytheistic enemies in Mecca. A similar story relates how

'Ali, the fourth caliph (ruler of the Muslim community) and Muhammad's son-in-law, followed Muhammad's advice to refrain from fighting until he had "the support of forty men." Some scholars interpret these legends as examples of *taqiyyah*. By avoiding combat against enemies of Islam until they could muster sufficient military force and moral support, 'Ali and Muhammad preserved not only their own lives but their divinely appointed mission to spread the faith.

Neither the Qur'an nor the Hadith decrees points of doctrine or prescribes guidelines for behaviour when using *taqiyyah*. The circumstances in which it may be used and the extent to which it is obligatory have been widely disputed by Islamic scholars. According to scholarly and judicial consensus, it is not justified by the threat of flogging, temporary imprisonment, or other relatively tolerable punishments. The danger to the believer must be unavoidable. Also, while *taqiyyah* may involve disguising or suppressing one's religious identity, it is not a license for a shallow profession of faith. Oaths taken with mental reservation, for example, are justified on the basis that God accepts what one believes inwardly. Consideration of community rather than private welfare is stressed in most cases.

marriage, called *mut'ah*, which can be legally contracted for a fixed period of time on the stipulation of a fixed dower.

From a spiritual point of view, perhaps the greatest difference between Shi'ism and Sunnism is the former's introduction into Islam of the passion motive, which is conspicuously absent from Sunni Islam. The violent death (in 680) of 'Ali's son, Husayn, at the hands of the Umayyad troops is celebrated with moving orations, passion plays, and processions in which the participants, in a state of emotional frenzy, beat their breasts with heavy chains and sharp instruments, inflicting wounds on their bodies. This passion motive has also influenced the Sunni masses in Afghanistan and the Indian subcontinent, where they

Muslims at a ta'ziyah, *a passion play commemorating the martyrdom of* Husayn, in Jaipur, India. Foto Features

participate in passion plays called *ta'ziyahs*. Such celebrations are, however, absent from Egypt and North Africa.

SUFISM

A third major influence on the development of Islam was the mystical movements together known as Sufism. Islamic mysticism is called *tasawwuf* (literally, "to dress in wool") in Arabic, but it has been called Sufism in Western languages since the early 19th century. An abstract word, Sufism derives from the Arabic term for a mystic, *sufi*, which is in turn derived from *suf*, "wool," plausibly a reference to the woolen garment of early Islamic ascetics. The Sufis are also generally known as "the poor," *fuqara'*, plural of the Arabic *faqir*, in Persian *darvish*, whence the English words fakir and dervish.

Though the roots of Islamic mysticism formerly were supposed to have stemmed from various non-Islamic sources in ancient Europe and even India, it now seems established that the movement grew out of early Islamic asceticism that developed as a counterweight to the increasing worldliness of the expanding Muslim community. Only later were foreign elements that were compatible with mystical theology and practices adopted and made to conform to Islam. By educating the masses and deepening the spiritual concerns of the Muslims, Sufism has played an important role in the formation of Muslim society. Opposed to the dry casuistry of the lawyer-divines, the mystics nevertheless scrupulously observed the commands of the divine law. The Sufis have been further responsible for a large-scale missionary activity all over the world, which still continues. Sufis have elaborated the image of the Prophet Muhammad and have thus largely influenced Muslim piety by their Muhammad-mysticism. Without the Sufi vocabulary, Persian and other literatures related to it, such as Turkish, Urdu, Sindhi, Pashto, and Panjabi, would lack their special charms. Through the poetry of these literatures mystical ideas spread widely among the Muslims. In some countries Sufi leaders were also active politically.

The first stage of Sufism appeared in pious circles as a reaction against the worldliness of the early Umayyad period (661–749). From their practice of constantly meditating on the Qur'anic words about Doomsday, the ascetics became known as "those who always weep" and those who considered this world "a hut of sorrows." They were distinguished by their scrupulous fulfillment of the injunctions

Members of the Sufi sect Cassanazaiyya chant as they fall into a trance at the Tarika Cassanazaiyyah Mosque in Baghdad, Iraq. There are fewer than 5 million Sufis in the Muslim world today. Marco Di Lauro/Getty Images

of the Qur'an and tradition, by many acts of piety, and especially by a predilection for night prayers.

Slightly later, mystical orders (fraternal groups cen-tring around the teachings of a leader-founder) began to crystallize. The 13th century, though politically overshad-owed by the invasion of the Mongols into the Eastern lands of Islam and the end of the 'Abbasid caliphate, was also the golden age of Sufism. The Spanish-born Ibn al-'Arabi created a comprehensive theosophical system concerning the relation of God and the world that was to become the cornerstone for a theory of "Unity of Being." According to this theory all existence is one, a manifestation of the underlying divine reality. His Egyptian contemporary Ibn al-Farid wrote the finest mystical poems in Arabic. Two other important mystics, who died *c.* 1220, were a Persian poet, Farid od-Din 'Attar, one of the most fertile writers on mystical topics, and a Central Asian master, Najmuddin Kubra, who presented elaborate discussions of the psychological experiences through which the mystic adept has to pass.

The greatest mystical poet in the Persian language, Jalal al-Din Rumi (1207–73), was moved by mystical love to compose his lyrical poetry that he attributed to his mystical beloved, Shams al-Din of Tabriz, as a symbol of their union. Rumi's didactic poem *Masnavi* in about 26,000 couplets—a work that is for the Persian-reading mystics second in importance only to the Qur'an—is an encyclopaedia of mystical thought in which everyone can find his own religious ideas. Rumi inspired the organization of the whirling dervishes—who sought ecstasy through an elaborate dancing ritual, accompanied by superb music. His younger contemporary Yunus Emre inaugurated Turkish mystical poetry with his charming verses that were transmitted by the Bektashiyah (Bektasi) order of dervishes and are still admired in modern Turkey. In Egypt, among many other mystical trends, an order—known as Shadhiliyah—was founded by al-Shadhili (died 1258); its main literary representative, Ibn 'Ata' Allah of Alexandria, wrote sober aphorisms (*hikam*).

During this time, the basic ideals of Sufism permeated the whole world of Islam. At its borders as, for example, in India, Sufis largely contributed to shaping Islamic society. Later some of the Sufis in India were brought closer to Hindu mysticism by an overemphasis on the idea of divine unity, which became almost monism—a religiophilosophic perspective according to which there is only one basic reality, and the distinction between God and the world (and man) tends to disappear. The syncretistic attempts of the Mughal emperor Akbar (died 1605) to combine different forms of belief and practice, and the religious discussions of the crown prince Dara Shukoh (executed for heresy, 1659) were objectionable to the orthodox. Typically, the countermovement was again undertaken by a mystical order, the Naqshbandiyah, a Central Asian fraternity founded in the 14th century. Contrary to the monistic trends of the school of *wahdat al-wujud* ("existential unity of being"), the later Naqshbandiyah defended the *wahdat al-shuhud* ("unity of vision"), a subjective experience of unity, occurring only in the mind of the believer, and not as an objective experience. Ahmad Sirhindi (died 1624) was the major protagonist of this movement in India. His claims of sanctity were surprisingly daring: he considered himself the divinely invested master of the universe. His refusal to concede the possibility of union between man and God (characterized as "servant" and "Lord") and his sober law-bound attitude gained him and his followers many disciples, even at the Mughal court and as far away as Turkey. In the 18th century, Shah Wali Allah of Delhi was connected with an attempt to reach a compromise between the two inimical schools of mysticism; he was also politically active and translated the Qur'an into Persian, the official language of Mughal India. Other Indian mystics of the 18th century, such as Mir Dard, played a decisive role in forming the newly developing Urdu poetry.

AL-GHAZALI

Abu Hamid Muhammad ibn Muhammad al-Tusi al-Ghazali (1058–1111) was an Islamic Muslim theologian and mystic whose great work, *Ihya' 'ulum al-din* ("The Revival of the Religious Sciences"), made Sufism (Islamic mysticism) an acceptable part of orthodox Islam.

During his appointment as chief professor in the Nizamiyah college in Baghdad, he passed through a spiritual crisis that rendered him physically incapable of lecturing for a time. In November 1095 he abandoned his academic career—an act that won him both followers and critics among his contemporaries—and left Baghdad on the pretext of going on pilgrimage to Mecca. Making arrangements for his family, he disposed of his wealth and adopted the life of a poor Sufi, or mystic. After some time in Damascus and Jerusalem, with a visit to Mecca in November 1096, al-Ghazali settled in Tus, where Sufi disciples joined him in a virtually monastic communal life. In 1106 he was persuaded to return to teaching at the Nizamiyah college at Nishapur. A consideration in this decision was that a "renewer" of the life of Islam was expected at the beginning of each century, and his friends argued that he was the "renewer" for the century beginning in September 1106. He continued lecturing in Nishapur at least until 1110, when he returned to Tus, where he died the following year.

More than 400 works are ascribed to al-Ghazali; at least 50 are known to be genuine. In al-Ghazali's greatest work, *Ihya' 'ulum al-din*, he explained the doctrines and practices of Islam and showed how these can be made the basis of a profound devotional life, leading to the higher stages of mysticism. The relation of mystical experience to other forms of cognition is discussed in *Mishkat al-anwar* (*The Niche for Lights*). Al-Ghazali's abandonment of his career and adoption of a mystical, monastic life is defended in the autobiographical work *al-Munqidh min al-dalal* ("The Deliverer from Error").

His philosophical studies began with treatises on logic and culminated in the *Tahafut* ("The Inconsistency—or Incoherence—of the Philosophers"), in which he defended Islam against such philosophers as Avicenna who sought to demonstrate certain speculative views contrary to accepted Islamic teaching. In preparation for this major treatise, he published an objective account of *Maqasid al-falasifah* ("The Aims of the Philosophers"). This book was influential in Europe and was one of the first to be translated from Arabic to Latin (12th century).

In the Arabic parts of the Islamic world, only a few interesting mystical authors are found after 1500. They include al-Sha'rani in Egypt (died 1565) and the prolific writer 'Abd al-Ghani an-Nabulusi in Syria (died 1731). Turkey produced some fine mystical poets in the 17th and 18th centuries. The influence of the mystical orders did not recede; rather new orders came into existence, and most literature was still tinged with mystical ideas and expressions. Political and social reformers in the Islamic countries have often objected to Sufism because they have generally considered it as backward, hampering the free development of society. Thus, the orders and dervish lodges in Turkey were closed by Kemal Atatürk in 1925. Yet, their political influence is still palpable, though under the surface. Such modern Islamic thinkers as the Indian philosopher Muhammad Iqbal have attacked traditional monist mysticism and have gone back to the classical ideals or divine love as expressed by Hallaj and his contemporaries. The activities of modern Muslim mystics in the cities are mostly restricted to spiritual education.

The mystics drew their vocabulary largely from the Qur'an, which for Muslims contains all divine wisdom and has to be interpreted with ever-increasing insight. In the Qur'an, mystics found the threat of the Last Judgment, but they also found the statement that God "loves them and they love him," which became the basis for love-mysticism. Strict obedience to the religious law and imitation of the Prophet were basic for the mystics. By rigid introspection and mental struggle the mystic tried to purify his baser self from even the smallest signs of selfishness, thus attaining *ikhlas*, absolute purity of intention and act. *Tawakkul* (trust in God) was sometimes practiced to such an extent that every thought of tomorrow was considered irreligious. "Little sleep, little talk, little food" were fundamental; fasting became one of the most important preparations for the spiritual life.

The central concern of the Sufis, as of every Muslim, was *tawhid*, the witness that "There is no deity but God." This truth had to be realized in the existence of each individual, and so the expressions differ. Early Sufism postulated the approach to God through love and voluntary suffering until a unity of will was reached. Junayd spoke of "recognizing God as He was before creation"; God is seen as the One and only actor; He alone "has the right to say 'I'." Later, *tawhid* came to mean the knowledge that there is nothing existent but God, or the ability to see God and creation as two aspects of one reality, reflecting each other and depending upon each other (*wahdat al-wujud*).

The mystics realized that beyond the knowledge of outward sciences intuitive knowledge was required in order to receive that illumination to which reason has no access. *Dhawq*, direct "tasting" of experience, was essential for them. But the inspirations and "unveilings" that God grants such mystics by special grace must never contradict the Qur'an and tradition and are valid only for the person concerned. Even the Malamatis, who attracted public contempt upon themselves by outwardly acting against the law, in private life strictly followed the divine commands. Mystics who expressed in their poetry their disinterest in, and even contempt of, the traditional formal religions never forgot that Islam is the highest manifestation of divine wisdom. The idea of the manifestation of divine wisdom was also connected with the person of the Prophet Muhammad. Though early Sufism had concentrated upon the relation between God and the soul, from 900 onward a strong Muhammad-mysticism developed. In the very early years, the alleged divine address to the Prophet—"If thou hadst not been I had not created the worlds"—was common among Sufis. Muhammad was said to be "Prophet when Adam was still between water and clay." Muhammad is also described as light from light, and from his light all the prophets are created, constituting the different aspects of this light. In its fullness such light radiated from the historical Muhammad and is partaken of by his posterity and by the saints; for Muhammad has the aspect of sanctity in addition to that of prophecy.

A mystic may also be known as *wali*. The word *wali* ("saint"), also means "one in close relation" or "friend." The *awliya'* (plural of *wali*) are "friends of God who have no fear nor are they sad." Later the term *wali* came to denote the Muslim mystics who had reached a certain stage of proximity to God, or those who had reached the highest mystical stages. They have their "seal" (i.e., the last and most perfect personality in the historical process; with this person, the evolution has found its end—as in Muhammad's case), just as the prophets have. Woman saints are found all over the Islamic world.

The invisible hierarchy of saints consists of the 40 *abdal* ("substitutes"; for when any of them dies another is elected by God from the rank and file of the saints), seven *awtad* ("stakes," or "props," of faith), three *nuqaba'* ("leader"; "one who introduces people to his master"), headed by the *qutb* ("axis, pole"), or *ghawth* ("help")—titles claimed by many Sufi leaders. Saint worship is contrary to Islam, which does not admit of any mediating role for human beings between man and God; but the cult of living and even more of dead saints—visiting their tombs to take vows there—responded to the feeling of the masses, and thus a number of pre-Islamic customs were absorbed into Islam under the cover of mysticism. The advanced mystic was often granted the capacity of working miracles called *karamat* (*charismata* or "graces"); not *mu'jizat* ("that which men are unable to imitate"), like the miracles of the prophets. Among them are "cardiognosia" (knowledge of the heart), providing food from the unseen, presence in two places at the same time, and help for the disciples, be they near or far. In short, a saint is one "whose prayers are heard" and who has *tasarruf*, the power of materializing in this world possibilities that still rest in the spiritual world. Many great saints, however, considered miracle working as a dangerous trap on the path that might distract the Sufi from his real goal.

The path (*tariqah*) begins with repentance. A mystical guide (*sheikh*, or *pir*) accepts the seeker as disciple (*murid*), orders him to follow strict ascetic practices, and suggests certain formulas for meditation. It is said that the disciple should be in the hands of the master "like a corpse in the hand of the washer." The master teaches him constant struggle (the real "Holy War") against the lower soul, often represented as a black dog, which should, however, not be killed but merely tamed and used in the way of God. The mystic dwells in a number of spiritual stations (*maqam*), which are described in varying sequence, and, after the initial repentance, comprise abstinence, renunciation, and poverty—according to Muhammad's saying, "Poverty is my pride." Poverty was sometimes interpreted as having no interest in anything apart from God, the Rich One, but the concrete meaning of poverty prevailed, which is why the mystic is often denoted as "poor," fakir or dervish. Patience and gratitude belong to higher stations of the path, and consent is the loving acceptance of every affliction.

On his way to illumination the mystic will undergo such changing spiritual states (*hal*) as *qabd* and *bast*, constraint and happy spiritual expansion, fear and hope, and longing and intimacy, which are granted by God and last for longer or shorter periods of time, changing in intensity according to the station in which the mystic is abiding at the moment. The way culminates in *ma'rifah* ("interior knowledge," "gnosis") or in *mahabbah* ("love"), the central subject of Sufism since the 9th century, which implies a union of lover and beloved, and was therefore violently rejected by the orthodox, for whom "love of God" meant simply obedience. The final goal is *fana'* ("annihilation"), primarily an ethical concept of annihilating one's own qualities, according to the prophetic saying "Take over the qualities of God," but slowly developing into a complete extinction of the personality. Some mystics taught that behind this negative unity where the self is completely effaced, the *baqa'*, ("duration, life in God") is found. The ecstatic experience, called intoxication, is followed by the "second sobriety"; i.e., the return of the completely transformed mystic into this world where he acts as a living witness of God or continues the "journey in God." The mystic has reached *haqiqah* ("reality"), after finishing the *tariqah* ("path"), which is built upon Shari'ah ("law"). Later, the disciple is led through *fana' fi ashshaykh* ("annihilation in the master") to *fana' fiar-Rasul* ("annihilation in the Prophet") before reaching, if at all, *fana' fi-Allah* ("annihilation in God").

One of the means used on the path is the ritual prayer, or *dhikr* ("remembrance"), derived from the Qur'anic injunction "And remember God often" (sura 62, verse 10). It consists in a repetition of either one or all of the most beautiful names of God, of the name "Allah," or of a certain religious formula, such as the profession of faith: "There is no God but Allah, and Muhammad is his prophet." The rosary with 99 or 33 beads was in use as early as the 8th century for counting the thousands of repetitions. Man's whole being should eventually be transformed into remembrance of God.

In the mid-9th century some mystics introduced sessions with music and poetry recitals (*sama*) in Baghdad in order to reach the ecstatic experience—and since then debates about the permissibility of *sama*, filling many books, have been written. Narcotics were used in periods of degeneration, coffee by the "sober" mystics (first by the Shadhiliyah after 1300).

Besides the wayfarers (*salik*) on the path, Sufis who have no master but are attracted solely by divine grace are also found. They are called Uwaysi, after Uways al-Qarani, the Yemenite contemporary of the Prophet who never saw him but firmly believed in him. There are also the so-called *majdhub* ("attracted") who are often persons generally agreed to be more or less mentally deranged.

The divine truth was at times revealed to the mystic in visions, auditions, and dreams, in colours and sounds, but to convey these nonrational and ineffable experiences to others the mystic had to rely upon such terminology of worldly experience as that of love and intoxication—often objectionable from the orthodox viewpoint. The symbolism of wine, cup, and cupbearer, first expressed by Abu Yazid al-Bistami in the 9th century, became popular everywhere, whether in the verses of the Arab Ibn al-Farid, or the Persian 'Iraqi, or the Turk Yunus Emre, and their followers. The hope for the union of the soul with the divine had to be expressed through images of human yearning and love. The love for lovely boys in which the divine beauty manifests itself—according to the alleged Hadith "I saw my Lord in the shape of a youth with a cap awry"—was commonplace in Persian poetry. Union was described as the submersion of the drop in the ocean, the state of the iron in the fire, the vision of penetrating light, or the burning of the moth in the candle (first used by Hallaj). Worldly phenomena were seen as black tresses veiling the radiant beauty of the divine countenance. The mystery of unity and diversity was symbolized, for example, under the image of mirrors that reflect the different aspects of the divine, or as prisms colouring the pure light. Every aspect of nature was seen in relation to God. The symbol of the soulbird—in which the human soul is likened to a flying bird—known everywhere, was the centre of 'Attar's *Manteq ot-teyr* ("The Birds' Conversation"). The predilection of the mystical poets for the symbolism of the nightingale (the soul) and the red rose (God's perfect beauty) stems from the soul-bird symbolism. For spiritual education, symbols taken from medicine (healing of the sick soul) and alchemy (changing of base matter into gold) were also used. Many descriptions that were originally applied to God as the goal of love were, in later times, used also for the Prophet, who is said to be like the "dawn between the darkness of the material world and the sun of Reality."

Allusions to the Qur'an were frequent, especially those verses that seem to imply divine immanence (God's presence in the world), such as "Whithersoever ye turn, there is the Face of God" (sura 2, verse 109), or that God is "Closer than your neck-vein" (sura 50:8). As for the prophets before Muhammad, the vision of Moses was considered still imperfect, for the mystic wants the actual vision of God, not His manifestation through a burning bush. Abraham, for whom fire turned into a rose garden, resembles the mystic in his afflictions; Joseph, in his perfect beauty, the mystical beloved after whom the mystic searches. The apocryphal traditions used by the mystics are numerous; such as "Heaven and earth do not contain me, but the heart of my faithful servant contains Me"; and the possibility of a relation between man and God is also explained by the traditional idea: "He (God) created Adam in His image."

Mystical life was first restricted to the relation between a master and a few disciples. The foundations of a monastic system were laid by the Persian Abu Sa'id ebn Abi ol-Kheyr (died 1049), but real orders or fraternities came into existence only from the 12th century onward: 'Abd al-Qadir al-Jilani (died 1166) gathered the first and still most important order around himself; then followed the Suhrawardiyah, and the 13th century saw the formation of large numbers of different orders in the East (for example, Kubrawiya in Khvarezm) and West (Shadhiliyah). Thus, Sufism ceased to be the way of the chosen few and influenced the masses. A strict ritual was elaborated: when the adept had found a master for whom he had to feel a pre-formed affinity, there was an initiation ceremony in which he swore allegiance (*bay'at*) into the master's hand. Similarities between this ritual and the initiation in Isma'ilism, the 9th-century sect, and in the guilds suggest a possible interaction. The disciple (*murid*) had to undergo a stern training. He was often ordered to perform the lowest work in the community, to serve the brethren, to go out to beg (many of the old monasteries subsisted upon alms). A seclusion period of 40 days under hard conditions was common for the adepts in most orders.

Investiture with the *khirqah*, the frock of the master, originally made from shreds and patches, was the decisive act by which the disciple became part of the *silsilah*, the chain of mystical succession and transmission, which leads back—via Junayd—to the Prophet himself and differs in every order. Some mystical leaders claimed to have received their *khirqah* directly from al-Khidr, a mysterious immortal saint.

In the earliest times, allegiance was sworn exclusively to one master who had complete power over the disciple, controlling each of his movements, thoughts, visions, and dreams; but later many Sufis got the *khirqah* from two or more *sheikhs*. There is consequently a differentiation between the *sheikh at-tarbiyah*, who introduces the disciple into the ritual, forms, and literature of the order, and the *sheikh as-suhbah*, who steadily watches him and with whom the disciple lives. Only a few members of the fraternity remained in the centre (*dargah, khanqah, tekke*), close to the *sheikh*, but even those were not bound to celibacy. Most of the initiated returned to their daily life and partook in mystic services only during certain periods. The most mature disciple was invested as *khali fah* ("successor") to the *sheikh* and was often sent abroad to extend the activities of the order. The *dargah*s were organized differently in the various orders. Some relied completely upon alms, keeping their members in utmost poverty; others were rich, and their *sheikh* was not very different from a feudal lord. Relations with rulers varied — some masters refused contacts with the representatives of political power; others did not mind friendly relations with the grandees.

Each order has peculiarities in its ritual. Most start the instruction with breaking the lower soul; others, such as the later Naqshbandiyah, stress the purification of the heart by constant *dhikr* ("remembrance") and by discourse with the master (*suhbah*). The forms of *dhikr* vary in the orders. Many of them use the word Allah, or the profession of faith with its rhythmical wording, sometimes accompanied by movements of the body, or by breath control up to complete holding of the breath. The Mawlawis, the whirling dervishes, are famous for their dancing ritual, an organized variation of the earlier *sama'* practices, which were confined to music and poetry. The Rifa'is, the so-called Howling Dervishes, have become known for their practice of hurting themselves while in an ecstatic state that they reach in performing their loud *dhikr*. (Such practices that might well degenerate into mere jugglery are not approved by most orders.) Some orders also teach the *dhikr khafi*, silent repetition of the formulas, and meditation, concentrating upon certain fixed points of the body; thus the Naqshbandis do not allow any emotional practices and prefer contemplation to ecstasy, perhaps as a result of Buddhist influence from Central Asia. Other orders have special prayers given to the disciples, such as the protective *hizb al-bahr* ("The protective armour of the sea"; i.e., for seafaring people — then extended to all travelers) in the Shadhiliyah order. Most of them prescribe for their disciples additional prayers and meditation at the end of each ritual prayer.

The orders formed an excellent means of bringing together the spiritually interested members of the community. They acted as a counterweight against the influence of hairsplitting lawyer-divines and gave the masses an emotional outlet in enthusiastic celebrations (*'urs*, "marriage") of the anniversaries of the deaths of founders of mystic orders or similar festivals in which they indulged in music and joy. The orders were adaptable to every social level; thus, some of them were responsible for adapting a number of un-Islamic folkloristic practices such as veneration of saints. Their way of life often differed so much from Islamic ideals that one distinguishes in Iran and India between orders *ba shar'* (law-bound) and *bi shar'* (not following the injunctions of the Qur'an). The figure of 'Ali played a role also in other fraternities, and the relations between Sufism in the 14th and 15th centuries and the Shi'ah still have to be explored, as is also true of the general influence of Shi'ite ideas on Sufism. Other orders, such as the Shadhiliyah, an offshoot of which still plays an important role among Egyptian officials and employees,

IBN AL-'ARABI

Ibn al-'Arabi (1165–1240), whose full name was Muhyi al-Din Abu 'Abd Allah Muhammad ibn 'Ali ibn Muhammad ibn al-'Arabi al-Hatimi al-Ta'i ibn al-'Arabi, was a celebrated Muslim mystic-philosopher who gave the esoteric, mystical dimension of Islamic thought its first full-fledged philosophic expression. His major works are the monumental *Al-Futuhat al-Makkiyyah* ("The Meccan Revelations") and *Fusus al-hikam* (1229; "The Bezels of Wisdom").

Ibn al-'Arabi was born in the southeast of Spain, a man of pure Arab blood whose ancestry went back to the prominent Arabian tribe of Ta'i. It was in Sevilla (Seville), then an outstanding centre of Islamic culture and learning, that he received his early education. He stayed there for 30 years, studying traditional Islamic sciences; he studied with a number of mystic masters who found in him a young man of marked spiritual inclination and unusually keen intelligence. During those years he traveled a great deal and visited various cities of Spain and North Africa in search of masters of the Sufi (mystical) Path who had achieved great spiritual progress and thus renown.

On one of these journeys Ibn al-'Arabi had a dramatic encounter with the great Aristotelian philosopher Ibn Rushd (Averroës; 1126–98) in the city of Córdoba. Averroës, a close friend of Ibn al-'Arabi's father, had asked that the interview be arranged because he had heard of the extraordinary nature of the young, still beardless lad. After the early exchange of only a few words, it is said, the mystical depth of the boy so overwhelmed the old philosopher that he became pale and, dumbfounded, began trembling. In the light of the subsequent course of Islamic philosophy the event is seen as symbolic; even more symbolic is the sequel of the episode, which has it that, when Averroës died, his remains were returned to Córdoba. The coffin that contained his remains was loaded on one side of a beast of burden, while the books written by him were placed on the other side in order to counterbalance it. It was a good theme of meditation and recollection for the young Ibn al-'Arabi, who said: "On one side the Master, on the other his books! Ah, how I wish I knew whether his hopes had been fulfilled!"

In 1198, while in Murcia, Ibn al-'Arabi had a vision in which he felt he had been ordered to leave Spain and set out for the East. Thus began his pilgrimage to the Orient, from which he never was to return to his homeland. The first notable place he visited on this journey was Mecca (1201), where he "received a divine commandment" to begin his major work *Al-Futuhat al-Makkiyyah* ("The Meccan Revelations"), which was to be completed much later in Damascus. In 560 chapters, it is a work of tremendous size, a personal encyclopaedia extending over all the esoteric sciences in Islam as Ibn al-'Arabi understood and had experienced them, together with valuable information about his own inner life.

It was also in Mecca that Ibn al-'Arabi became acquainted with a young girl of great beauty who, as a living embodiment of the eternal *sophia* (wisdom), was to play in his life a role much like that which Beatrice played for Dante. Her memories were eternalized by Ibn al-'Arabi in a collection of love poems (*Tarjuman al-ashwaq*; "The Interpreter of Desires"), upon which he himself composed a mystical commentary. His daring "pantheistic" expressions drew down on him the wrath of Muslim orthodoxy, some of whom prohibited the reading of his works at the same time that others were elevating him to the rank of the prophets and saints.

After Mecca, Ibn al-'Arabi visited Egypt (also in 1201) and then Anatolia, where, in Qonya, he met Sadr al-Din al-Qunawi, who was to become his most important follower and successor in the East. From Qonya he went on to Baghdad and Aleppo (modern Halab, Syria). By the time his long pilgrimage had come to an end at Damascus (1223), his fame had spread all over the Islamic world. Venerated as the greatest spiritual master, he spent the rest of his life in Damascus in peaceful contemplation, teaching, and writing. It was during his Damascus days that one of the most important works in mystical philosophy in Islam, *Fusus al-hikam* ("The Bezels of Wisdom"), was composed in 1229, about 10 years before his death. Consisting of only 27 chapters, the book is incomparably smaller than *Al-Futuhat al-Makkiyyah*, but its importance as an expression of Ibn al-'Arabi's mystical thought in its most mature form cannot be overemphasized.

are typically middle class. This order demands not a life in solitude but strict adherence to one's profession and fulfillment of one's duty.

The main contribution of the orders, however, is their missionary activity. The members of different orders who settled in India from the early 13th century attracted thousands of Hindus by their example of love of both God and their own brethren and by preaching the equality of men. Missionary activity was often joined with political activity, as in 17th- and 18th-century Central Asia, where the Naqshbandiyah exerted strong political influence. In North Africa the Tijaniyah, founded in 1781, and the Sanusiyah, active since the early 19th century, both heralded Islam and engaged in politics. The Sanusiyah fought against Italy, and the former king of Libya was the head of the order. The Tijaniyah extended the borders of Islam toward Senegal and Nigeria, and their representatives founded large kingdoms in West Africa. Their influence, as well as that of the Qadiriyah, is still an important sociopolitical factor in those areas.

Sufism has helped to shape large parts of Muslim society. The orthodox disagree with such aspects of Sufism as saint worship, visiting of tombs, musical performances, miracle mongering, degeneration into jugglery, and the adaptation of pre-Islamic and un-Islamic customs. The reformers object to the influences of the monistic interpretation of Islam upon moral life and human activities. The importance given to the figure of the master is accused of yielding negative results; the *sheikh* as the almost infallible leader of his disciples and admirers could gain dangerous authority and political influence, for the illiterate villagers in backward areas used to rely completely upon the "saint." Yet, other masters have raised their voices against social inequality and have tried, even at the cost of their lives, to change social and political conditions for the better and to spiritually revive the masses. The missionary activities of the Sufis have enlarged the fold of the faithful. The importance of Sufism for spiritual education, and inculcation in the faithful of the virtues of trust in God, piety, faith in God's love, and veneration of the Prophet, cannot be overrated. The *dhikr* formulas still preserve their consoling and quieting power even for the illiterate. Mysticism permeates Persian literature and other literatures influenced by it. Such poetry has always been a source of happiness for millions, although some modernists have disdained its "narcotic" influence on Muslim thinking.

Industrialization and modern life have led to a constant decrease in the influence of Sufi orders in many countries. The spiritual heritage is preserved by individuals who sometimes try to show that mystical experience conforms to modern science. Today in the West, Sufism is popularized, but the genuinely and authentically devout are aware that it requires strict discipline, and that its goal can be reached—if at all—as they say, only by throwing oneself into the consuming fire of divine love.

WAHHABISM

A small but influential puritan movement exists in Islam known as Wahhabi. Founded by Muhammad ibn 'Abd al-Wahhab (1703–1792) in the 18th century in Najd, central Arabia, and adopted in 1744 by the Sa'udi family, the Wahhabi attempted a return to the "true" principles of Islam. The political fortunes of the Wahhabi were immediately allied to those of the Sa'udi dynasty. By the end of the 18th century, they had brought all of Najd under their control, attacked Karbala', Iraq, a holy city of the Shi'ite branch of Islam, and occupied Mecca and Medina in western Arabia. The Ottoman sultan brought an end to the first Wahhabi empire in 1818, but the sect revived under the leadership of the Sa'udi Faysal I. The empire was then somewhat restored until once again destroyed at the end of the 19th century by the Rashidiyah of northern Arabia. The activities of Ibn Sa'ud in the 20th century eventually led to the creation of the Kingdom of Saudi Arabia in 1932 and assured the Wahhabi religious and political dominance on the Arabian Peninsula.

The term Wahhabi is generally used by non-Muslims and opponents. Members of the Wahhabi call themselves al-Muwahhidun, "Unitarians," a name derived from their emphasis on the absolute oneness of God (*tawhid*). They deny all acts implying polytheism, such as visiting tombs and venerating saints, and advocate a return to the original teachings of Islam as incorporated in the Qur'an and Hadith, with condemnation of all innovations (*bid'ah*). Wahhabi theology and jurisprudence, based, respectively, on the teachings of Ibn Taymiyah and on the legal school of Ahmad ibn Hanbal, stress literal belief in the Qur'an and Hadith and the establishment of a Muslim state based only on Islamic law.

Having completed his formal education in the holy city of Medina, in Arabia, 'Abd al-Wahhab lived abroad for many years. He taught for four years in Basra, Iraq, and in Baghdad he married an affluent woman whose property he inherited when she died. In 1736, in Iran, he began to teach against what he considered to be the extreme ideas of various exponents of Sufi doctrines. On returning to his native city, he wrote the *Kitab at-tawhid* ("Book of Unity"), which is the main text for Wahhabi doctrines.

'Abd al-Wahhab's teachings have been characterized as puritanical and traditional, representing the early era of the Islamic religion. He made a clear stand against all (*bid'ah*) in Islamic faith because he believed them to be

King Ibn Sa'ud, born in Riyadh in 1876, followed his family into exile in 1890. Twelve years later he attacked and took back Riyadh. As he worked to consolidate control over the Arabian Peninsula he also revived Wahhabism. John Philips/Time & Life Pictures/Getty Images

reprehensible, insisting that the original grandeur of Islam could be regained if the Islamic community would return to the principles enunciated by the Prophet Muhammad. Wahhabi doctrines, therefore, do not allow for an intermediary between the faithful and Allah and condemn any such practice as polytheism. The decoration of mosques, the cult of saints, and even the smoking of tobacco were condemned. When the preaching of these doctrines led to controversy, 'Abd al-Wahhab was expelled from 'Uyaynah in 1744. He then settled in Ad-Dir'iyah, capital of Ibn Sa'ud, a ruler of the Najd (now in Saudi Arabia).

The spread of Wahhabism originated from the alliance that was formed between 'Abd al-Wahhab and Ibn Sa'ud, who, by initiating a campaign of conquest that was continued by his heirs, made Wahhabism the dominant force in Arabia since 1800. Propagating the doctrines of 'Abd al-Wahhab, Ibn Sa'ud and his son mastered all Najd. Late in the 18th century the Wahhabis began raiding Iraq and then besieged Mecca, which they definitively conquered in 1806. The Ottomans became so alarmed at the Sa'udi-Wahhabi peril that they urged Muhammad 'Ali, viceroy of Egypt, to drive the Wahhabis from the Holy Cities. Egyptian troops invaded Arabia, and after a bitter seven-year struggle the viceroy's forces recaptured Mecca and Medina. The Wahhabi leader was forced to surrender his capital and was then beheaded. Egyptian occupation of western Arabia continued some 20 years.

The second Sa'udi-Wahhabi kingdom began when Turki, of a collateral Sa'udi branch, revolted and in 1824 captured Riyadh in Najd and made it his capital. He was succeeded by his son Faysal. By 1833 Wahhabi overlordship was generally recognized in the Persian Gulf, though the Egyptians remained in the Hejaz.

After Faysal's death the fratricidal ambitions of his two eldest sons allowed Ibn Rashid, ruler of Ha'il in Jabal Shammar to the north, to take Riyadh. Ibn Rashid ruled northern Arabia until he died in 1897. Meanwhile, the Sa'udis in 1871 had lost the fertile Al-Hasa to the

Ottoman Turks, and the family ultimately took refuge in nearby Kuwait.

Ibn Rashid's son and successor became involved in a struggle with the *sheikh* of Kuwait, which enabled the greatest of the Sa'udis, Ibn Sa'ud ('Abd al-'Aziz II), to retake Riyadh in 1902 and establish the third Sa'udi kingdom. By 1904, through raiding and skirmishing, Ibn Sa'ud had recovered much of the earlier Sa'udi territory. In 1912, to bring the nomads under control, he set up agricultural settlements colonized by Wahhabi warrior groups called Ikhwan.

When World War I broke out, Kuwait renounced allegiance to the Ottoman Empire. Ibn Sa'ud fought the pro-Ottoman Rashidis but otherwise remained inactive. During the war, relations between Sharif Husayn and Ibn Sa'ud worsened. In 1919 the dispute broke into an open clash. The Wahhabis won so decisive a victory that they might have advanced unopposed into the Hejaz but for pressures on Ibn Sa'ud by the British. Instead, Ibn Sa'ud concentrated his forces against Ibn Rashid, mastering all Shammar territory and capturing Ha'il in 1921.

Meanwhile, the grand sharif refused the terms of a treaty with Britain, mainly because of the Balfour Declaration, which approved a national home in Palestine for the Jews. The Wahhabis marched into the Hejaz in 1924, and by October Husayn was ruler no longer. Ibn Sa'ud's zealous Wahhabi followers, arriving in the more cosmopolitan atmosphere of Hejaz society, were now exposed to the world of Islam at large. Ibn Sa'ud managed the resulting problems with firmness and tact. He had furthermore to enforce his rule over the tribes impatient with centralized government. His tough action with them won, and he set out to develop security, economic reform, and communications. On Ibn Sa'ud's southern border the Idrisi sayyids of Asir had risen to power in the first decade of the 20th century. When in 1926 and 1930 Ibn Sa'ud concluded agreements with the Idrisi, rendering Asir a virtual dependency of Saudi Arabia, Imam Yahya of Yemen took Al-Hudaydah and southern Asir. Saudi troops swept into the Yemeni Tihamah, but they withdrew after the Treaty of Al-Ta'if in 1934, which acknowledged Saudi rule over Asir.

ISLAMIC BELIEFS AND PRACTICES TODAY

Islam is one of the world's fastest growing religions today, with more than a billion followers worldwide. While some elements of Islam have remained unchanged since the time of Muhammad, like most religions, it continues to evolve to meet the needs of its many and varied followers.

GLOSSARY

abhorrence Extreme dislike.

ablution A cleansing of the body, particularly as a religious rite.

anthropomorphism Giving human characteristics to something that is not human.

apocalyptic Revealing hidden, often divine knowledge; popularly used to mean prophetic of imminent disaster.

apostate A person who abandons his religion, political party, or principles.

attestation Declaration.

caliphate The political leadership of a Muslim state.

canonical Authorized, conforming to established rules.

catholicity Universality.

concupiscent Covetous.

contemporaneous Happening during the same time.

corporeal Taking bodily form; tangible.

dichotomy Divided into two contradictory parts.

egalitarianism A doctrine of the equality of all mankind.

entourage A group following an important person.

eschatological Dealing with the ultimate destiny of the world and mankind.

esoteric Confined to a small group, private.

exegesis Critical analysis of a text, especially a religious text.

fait accompli An accomplished fact; something already done.

filial The relationship of a child to a parent.

genealogy The study of ancestry.

heretical Against the teaching of official religious doctrine.

incumbent Necessary as a responsibility.

ineffable Inexpressible.

infanticide The murder of a newborn.

investiture The ceremony of putting someone into office.

latitudinarianism Holding broad, tolerant views.

muezzin The Muslim official who proclaims the call to prayer.

mysticism Spiritual practices and disciplines enabling the acquisition of knowledge about ultimate or divine truth.

nomad A person who has no permanent home and instead moves about from place to place.

nonlinear Not in a straight line.

omnipotence Having unlimited power and authority.

onerous Burdensome.

paganism Religion based on local rituals, often including polytheistic idol worship.

piety Intense religious devotion.

pluralistic The theory of having more than one basic principle.

polemical Controversial.

polygyny Having more than one wife at a time; polygamy.

polytheism Worshipping multiple gods.

primordial Existing in the beginning.

puritanical Rigidly conservative.

retrogress To move backward.

scion A descendant.

secularist One believing that religion should be separated from public affairs.

variegated Diverse.

zenith The highest point.

FOR FURTHER READING

Ahmed, Akbar. *Journey into Islam: The Crisis of Globalization*. Washington, DC: Brookings Institution Press, 2007.

Armstrong, Karen. *Islam: A Short History*. New York, NY: Modern Library, 2002.

Armstrong, Karen. *Muhammad: A Prophet for Our Time*. New York, NY: HarperCollins, 2006.

Berry, Donald Lee. *Pictures of Islam*. Macon, GA: Mercer University Press, 2007.

Dudley, William, ed. *Islam: Opposing Viewpoints*. San Diego, CA: Greenhaven Press, 2004.

Esposito, John L. *What Everyone Needs to Know About Islam*. New York, NY: Oxford University Press, 2002.

Gartenstein-Ross, Daveed. *My Year Inside Radical Islam: A Memoir*. New York, NY: Penguin, 2007.

Gehrke-White, Donna. *The Face Behind the Veil: The Extraordinary Lives of Muslim Women in America*. New York, NY: Citadel Press, 2006.

Haleem, M. A. S. Abdel. *The Qur'an*. New York, NY: Oxford University Press, 2008.

Lewis, Bernard, and Buntzie Ellis Churchill. *Islam: The Religion and the People*. Indianapolis, IN: Wharton Press, 2009.

Lings, Martin. *Muhammad: His Life Based on the Earliest Sources*. Rochester, NY: Inner Traditions International, 2006.

Morgan, Michael Hamilton. *Lost History: The Enduring Legacy of Muslim Scientists, Thinkers, and Artists.* Washington, DC: National Geographic, 2007.

Riley-Smith, Jonathan. *The Crusades, Christiantiy, and Islam.* New York, NY: Columbia University Press, 2008.

Rogerson, Barnaby. *The Heirs of Muhammad: Islam's First Century and the Origins of the Sunni-Shia Split.* Woodstock, NY: Overlook Press, 2007.

Schwartz, Stephen. *The Other Islam: Sufism and the Road to Global Harmony.* New York, NY: Doubleday, 2008.

INDEX

Jewish tribes, 34
Jews, 27, 30, 33, 34, 35, 36, 86,
    89, 130
jihad, 58, 71, 89, 90, 93–94
Judaism, 9, 44, 45
Julian calendar, 31

K

Karbala', Iraq, 173
Khadijah bint al-Khuwaylid,
    23, 25, 26
Khalid ibn al-Walid, 33, 35
Khomeini, Ruhollah, 149–150
Khosrow II, 35
Kitchener, Horatio Herbert, 57
Kubra, Najmuddin, 157
Kufa, 42

L

Last Day, 52, 53
laws, religious, 13, 44, 59, 62, 72,
    88, 110–127, 151–152, 174
    doctrines of, 111, 113, 118
    interpretation of (*ijtihad*),
        111, 113, 124, 126
    scholarly consensus of
        (*ijma'*), 113
    schools of, 118, 134
    types of, 118, 123–124
    usul al-fiqh, 113–114

M

Madinat al-Nabi, 11, 29, 141
mahdi, 14, 54, 55, 56, 57
Mahmud II, 104–105
al-Ma'mun, 58, 98

Mani, 130
Manichaeans, 130, 132
al-Mansur, 98
marriage, 60, 105, 106, 123,
    124–126, 153
Marwan II, 98
Masjid al-Nabi, 30
Masnavi, 157
al-Maturidi, 138, 139
Mecca, 9–10, 13, 20, 21, 22, 24,
    25, 26, 27, 28, 30, 32, 34, 35,
    36, 41, 42, 68, 73, 75, 79, 81,
    83, 109, 133, 152, 159, 171,
    173, 176
Medina, 12, 29, 30, 33, 34, 35,
    60, 75, 88, 95, 109, 110, 114,
    116, 132, 133, 137, 140, 141,
    173, 176
Mehmed VI Vahideddin, 105
millennialism, 55, 58
Mi'raj, 11, 26, 27, 28–29
Mirza 'Ali Mohammad of
    Shiraz, 57
Mohammad Reza Shah
    Pahlavi, 149
monasticism, 105, 159
monogamy, 106
monotheism, 32
Moses, 27, 28
mosque, 11, 30, 79, 144
    Jami' Mosque, 68
    Ka'bah (Great Mosque), 10, 11,
        20–21, 22, 24, 25, 34, 36, 46,
        73, 74, 79, 80, 81
    Mosque of the Prophet, 30
    structure of, 79–80
Mu'awiyah I, 95, 97, 142, 143, 144
Mughal Empire, 103
muhajirun, 30, 31, 35

29.75   3/31/10

LONGWOOD PUBLIC LIBRARY
800 Middle Country Road
Middle Island, NY 11953
(631) 924-6400
mylpl.net

LIBRARY HOURS

Monday-Friday	9:30 a.m. - 9:00 p.m.
Saturday	9:30 a.m. - 5:00 p.m.
Sunday (Sept-June)	1:00 p.m. - 5:00 p.m.